BORDEN CHANTRY

They all heard the shot.
It was at some distance off, but it had a clear, distinct retort that cut across their conversation, stilling their tongues, leaving them staring.

Shots were not uncommon at night, occasionally in the daytime, but rarely . . . before the drinkers got well started and after the hunters had come in . . .

But there was something about that shot that hit them all, and for a moment they just stared, frightened and wondering.

Borden Chantry got up and went outside. He knew it as well as if he'd seen it happen.

Somebody else was dead.

Bantam Books by Louis L'Amour

Ask your bookseller for the books you have missed

BENDIGO SHAFTER
BORDEN CHANTRY
BRIONNE
THE BROKEN GUN
THE BURNING HILLS
THE CALIFORNIOS
CALLAGHEN
CATLOW
CHANCY
CONAGHER
DARK CANYON
DOWN THE LONG HILLS
THE EMPTY LAND
FAIR BLOWS THE WIND
FALLON
THE FERGUSON RIFLE
THE FIRST FAST DRAW
FLINT
GUNS OF THE TIMBER-
  LANDS
HANGING WOMAN
  CREEK
THE HIGH GRADERS
HIGH LONESOME
HOW THE WEST WAS
  WON
THE IRON MARSHAL
THE KEY-LOCK MAN
KID RODELO
KILLOE
KILRONE
KIOWA TRAIL
THE MAN CALLED
  NOON
THE MAN FROM
  SKIBBEREEN
MATAGORDA
THE MOUNTAIN
  VALLEY WAR
NORTH TO THE RAILS
OVER ON THE DRY SIDE

THE PROVING TRAIL
THE QUICK AND THE
  DEAD
RADIGAN
REILLY'S LUCK
THE RIDER OF LOST
  CREEK
RIVERS WEST
SHALAKO
SILVER CANYON
SITKA
TAGGART
TUCKER
UNDER THE SWEET-
  WATER RIM
WAR PARTY
WESTWARD THE TIDE
WHERE THE LONG GRASS
  BLOWS

Sackett Titles by
Louis L'Amour

LOUIS L'AMOUR

BORDEN CHANTRY

BANTAM BOOKS · LONDON
TORONTO · NEW YORK

To
TOM
and
Jose—

BORDEN CHANTRY
A Bantam Book | October 1977
2nd printing .. November 1977   4th printing .... May 1978
3rd printing .... March 1978   5th printing ...... January 1979
6th printing ...... November 1979
7th printing

ISBN 0-553-13704-2

Published simultaneously in the United States and Canada

Bantam Books are published by Bantam Books, Inc. Its trade-
mark, consisting of the words "Bantam Books" and the por-
trayal of a bantam, is Registered in U.S. Patent and Trademark
Office and in other countries. Marca Registrada. Bantam
Books, Inc., 666 Fifth Avenue, New York, New York 10019.

PRINTED IN THE UNITED STATES OF AMERICA

Chapter I

Dawn came like a ghost to the silent street, a gray, dusty street lined with boardwalks, hitching rails and several short lengths of water trough. False-fronted buildings alternated with others of brick or stone, some with windows showing goods for sale, some blank and empty.

A door slammed, a well pump came to life, complaining in rusty accents, then a rooster crowed . . . answered by another from across the town.

Into the end of the street rode a lone cowboy on a crow-bait horse. He saw the sign of the Bon-Ton Restaurant, and turned toward it, then his horse shied and he saw the body of a man lying beside the walk.

He glanced at it, dismounted, then tied his horse at the rail. He tried the restaurant door and had started to turn away when the sound of footsteps drew him back. The door opened and a pleasant voice said, "Come in. There's coffee, breakfast ready in a few minutes."

"I ain't in no hurry." The cowboy straddled a chair, accepting the coffee. "Dead man out in the street."

"Again? Third this week. You just wait until Saturday. Saturday night's when they let the wolves howl. You stick around."

"I seen it here and yonder. Ain't figurin' on it. I'm ridin' over to Carson an' the steam cars." He jerked his head toward the street. "You seen him?"

"No . . . don't aim to. I seen a dead man. I seen two dozen of them, time to time. Ain't nothin' about bein' dead pleases me. Some drunken fight, no doubt. Happens all the time."

A woman came along the street, her heels clicking on the boardwalk. She passed the dead man, glanced back, then turned her head away and walked on to the post office.

1

A man crossing the street turned aside and bending over the dead man took the head by the hair and turned the face around. "Him? Prob'ly had it comin'," he said, and walked on.

Down the street another door slammed and somebody sang, off-key, of the streets of Laredo. Another pump started to squeak.

Finally the woman emerged from the post office, glanced at the body, then went to the door of the marshal's office and rapped vigorously.

"Borden? Borden? Are you in there?"

A tall, young man came to the door, slipping a suspender over his shoulder. "What's the matter, Prissy? You outa stamps?"

"There's a dead man lying in the street, Borden Chantry, and it's a disgrace. It . . . why, you should be ashamed! And you call yourself a marshal!"

"Wasn't even here last night, ma'am. I was clean over on the Picketwire. Prob'ly just some drunken shootin'."

"No matter what it was, Borden Chantry, you get that body out of the street! What's this town coming to, anyway? Dead bodies lying around, shootings and stabbings every night. You call yourself a marshal!"

"No, ma'am, I don't. The city council does. I only figured to be a rancher until that norther came along. Why, I was fixin' to be a rich man come spring!"

"You an' how many others? You get that body up, Borden, or I'll have the committee on you."

Borden Chantry chuckled. "Now, now, Prissy, you wouldn't do that, would you? Why, those old biddies—"

"Hush your mouth, Borden! If they heard you speak of them like that, why—!" She turned around and went back to the post office.

A tall, handsome man with sandy hair stopped on the walk across the street. "What's the matter, Bord? You in trouble?"

"Seems like. There's a body in the street an' our postmistress is reading the riot act over it. You'd think she'd never seen a dead man . . . at her age."

"Less you say about age to her, the better off you'll

be, Bord." He glanced at the body. "Who is it? Some drunk?"

"Prob'ly. I never did see so many men couldn't handle liquor. They get to drinkin' that block an' tackle whiskey and right away there's trouble."

"Block an' tackle whiskey?"

"Sure," Chantry chuckled at the old joke. "One drink an' you'll walk a block an' tackle anything!"

"Had breakfast, Bord? You get him off to the barn an' come on in. I'll stake you to some ham and eggs."

"All right, Lang. You just hold your horses. I'll get Big Injun. He'll tote him off for me."

Langdon Adams crossed the walk and entered the Bon-Ton, seating himself at a table near the window. It was a small town but a good town, and he was at home here. It was one place he really wanted to stay, for despite the occasional brawls between cowmen and miners, it was a pleasant enough town.

He watched the old Indian back a buckboard up to the hitching rail and then saw Borden Chantry and the Indian load the dead man into the back. The Indian drove off and Borden dusted his hands off and came inside.

A fat, buxom woman came in from the kitchen. "Here! You boys start on this. Ed's fixin' some more ham an' eggs. Why, we had a cowboy in here this morning that et enough for three! I never did see such a man!"

Borden Chantry walked through to the kitchen and poured water from a bucket into a wash-pan and rinsed his hands.

"Who was he?" Ed turned from the fire, spatula in hand. "Know him?"

"Never saw him before, Ed. Nice-lookin' feller, though. He surely doesn't look the part."

Borden Chantry walked between the tables to the one near the window.

Langdon Adams looked up, smiling. "Well, how does it feel to the marshal of a cowtown?"

"Don't care much for it, Lang. I'd rather be ranching, but I will say the city fathers were mighty nice to offer me the job. I was really wiped out."

"You and how many others? I never did see so many big men become small overnight. I was lucky. I hadn't many cattle and they were down yonder in the breaks and out of the wind. I don't think I lost over three or four head."

"Neither did Blossom. That widow-woman makes about as few mistakes as anybody I know. She trimmed her herds down, sold off all her scrub stuff, only kept good, sturdy stock that could last through, and they did."

"She's a fine woman."

Borden glanced at his friend. "You really shinin' up to her? Can't says I blame you. She's a mighty pretty woman, and she's got the best ranch left around here. And if you buy the old Williams place—"

"I haven't bought it yet. I'm not even sure if I want it."

"What? If you had that ranch, right next to hers, and then you two got married, you'd have about thirty sections of the best grazing in the state all to yourselves."

Ed brought the ham and eggs himself, then refilled their cups. He sat down, straddling a chair. "You catch that horse thief, Borden?"

"Uh-huh. He made him a good run, but I got him. He stole those two mares of Hyatt's. He couldn't have done worse. Why, there isn't two horses in the state look like them, or have their quality. Worst of it was, ever'body in this part of the country knows those mares. Hyatt Johnson's talked them up so much, and showed them around . . . A man would have to be a damn fool or a stranger to steal them."

"Well, which was he?"

"A stranger. He surely doesn't talk like any damn fool," Chantry commented. "I come up on this camp just shy of daybreak and waited until he rolled out of bed and went into the brush. Then I just stepped up and taken his gun belt and rifle and set there a-waitin' when he come back. He was mighty upset."

"Anybody got away since you been marshal, Bord?" Ed asked curiously.

"No . . . but there ain't been but four or five I had to go after. A man steals something, I try to get him. If a man kills somebody and then cuts and runs, I take in after him and bring him back for a hearing. If a man tried to prosecute every man who has a shooting or a knifing against him, there'd be nobody in town but the preacher, an'—"

"Preacher?" Ed scoffed. "You just don't know the preacher. He's had him a few scraps here and there."

"Well . . . I don't know about that. As long as it's a stand-off fight, nobody cares, and I certainly don't feel like trying to bring a man before a judge when the jury will surely turn him loose. Killing a man in a fair fight is about the safest thing you can do around here."

"Want to take a ride down to my place, Bord? Might get some wild turkeys."

"No . . . no, thanks, Lang. I got to see to this body. Get him identified and bury him, if there's no relatives."

"How many have relatives that show up?" Lang asked.

"One in ten. If you find out where their family's at they usually just say to bury him and send them whatever he left . . . which isn't much after a night or two boozing it up down to Henry's."

"Why bother? Seems a kind of thankless job to me. Just so as they get a Christian burial it should be enough. The town can't afford it."

"Costs only a coupla bucks, Lang. A blanket to bury him in if he hasn't one of his own, and somebody to dig the grave. Comes to that, I've dug nine graves so far this season, dug 'em myself."

They ate in silence. After a moment, Langdon Adams asked, "Bord, have you thought of going to Hyatt Johnson for a loan? To get started again, I mean. He knows you're a good cattleman, and he just might come up with the money."

"You've got to be joking. Money goes into that bank of Hyatt's. It doesn't come out. Anyway, I'll make my own start when I can. I won't be beholden to any man, nor work half of my life to pay no banker."

The door opened and a short, wiry man slouched in, unshaven, the hair under his narrow-brimmed hat uncombed and still showing fragments of straw from the barn where he had slept.

He sat down at a table, almost falling into the chair, then crossed his arms and leaned his head on his arms.

Ed came in and put a cup of coffee in front of him. "Johnny? Here she is. Y' look like y' need it. Drink up."

Johnny lifted his head and stared at the chef. "Thanks, Ed. Been a long time since the ol' Slash Seven days."

"It surely has. You want some flapjacks, Johnny?"

The drunk shook his head. "Stomach wouldn't hold 'em. Maybe later, Ed. Thanks." He gulped the last of his coffee and staggered out to the street.

Ed looked over at them. "Y' wouldn't know it now, but that there was the best puncher in this country when I come in here. That was six year back. He could ride anything wore hair, and was a better than fair hand with a rope, but he just can't handle whiskey."

"Top hand. Any outfit be glad to have him on the payroll. Now he couldn't get a job anywheres."

"Does he ever pay for the grub you give him?" Langdon asked skeptically. "I didn't see any money."

"He doesn't need it here," Ed replied shortly. "I like Johnny. He lent me a hand time an' again when I first hit this country, and never mentioned it.

"He was in a poker game, settin' around a blanket with some other punchers. I was sort of standin' by. Flat broke, no eatin' money. No job.

"I ast them if any knew where there was work, and they said no, an' I said I had to find a job pretty quick for I was sure enough broke.

"Johnny, he just reached over to his stack of money and taken off two or three bills and handed 'em to me. 'There's eatin' money till you make it,' he said. I made out to thank him an' he just waved me off.

"A couple of days later he slipped me three bucks on the street, and when I got a job, I paid him back."

"I know," Borden Chantry said, "Johnny was a good man . . . one of the best."

Langdon Adams pushed back his chair. "If you change your mind, Bord, come on out. We could shoot some turkeys and I'd show you the place."

"Maybe. I haven't seen Bess yet. I came in late and rather than wake them up I slept in the office. If I come in late and wake her up she doesn't get back to sleep."

Adams went out, and Ed brought a cup of coffee to the table. "Got any idea who that dead man was?"

"No, Ed. Some drunken cowboy, I guess. They will drink too much and get into arguments with the miners. Some of those Mexicans are tough . . . And then there's so many drifters coming through. Since the war there's a lot of footloose men who can't seem to find a place to light.

"As long as they shoot each other, nobody much cares, at least so long as it's a fair fight. Nobody likes murder or back-shooting, but there hasn't been one of those around here in years."

"Not since George Riggins was marshal. He had one ▸ . . least, I always figured it for murder. Far as that goes, Helen Riggins always figured the marshal was murdered."

"I wasn't around when that happened."

"Rock fell on him. He was ridin' some rough country out yonder, an' was close under a cliff. Three days before they found him."

"That dead man . . . did you see him around?"

"If it's the same one, he came in here to eat. Quiet man." Ed scowled. "Borden, that man didn't size up like no trouble-hunter. Quiet man, like I say. He sat alone, ate his meal and left."

"Pay for it?"

"Twenty-dollar gold piece. I give him change." Ed pushed back his chair and got up. "I got to clean up. Dot ain't comin' in today. Headache or somethin'. Sure is hard to get help . . . women-folks is always ailin' when you need 'em most."

Borden Chantry walked out on the street. He should go home, let Bess know he was back, anyway. She always worried whenever he rode out after outlaws, but so far it had proved less dangerous than handling wild horses or longhorns.

He'd go home, but first he'd stop by the old barn and have a look at the dead man. He didn't care for the job, but it was his to do, and he had to make a show of doing it. He told himself that, yet at the same time he knew he had never done anything just for show. He was no marshal. He'd never figured on being a law officer, but as long as they'd given him the job he'd do the best he could.

It was gloomy in the old barn. The body was laid out on an old worktable. The place smelled of moldy hay, and light came in through various cracks in the siding and roof.

Big Injun sat down against one wall, a tall old man in a high-crowned, undented black hat with a feather in it, a black shirt and worn blue pants made for a smaller man.

Borden Chantry walked across the dirt floor strewn with straw and looked down at the dead man.

A handsome man he had been . . . maybe thirty years old, could be younger or older. Not shabby. Face still, taut, brown from sun and wind. An outdoors man, a rider, by the look of him. Certainly no booze-fighter. Chantry glanced with interest at the large-roweled, many-pronged spurs. They were silver, with little bells.

Nothing like that around here, for they looked south-western . . . Mexican, maybe, or Californian. Most of the hands around right now were Wyoming or Montana hands . . . or from Kansas.

Gently, not to disturb the body, he went through the pockets. Three gold eagles . . . a handful of change. A red bandana handkerchief . . . no papers of any kind.

Removing the thong from the gun hammer, he drew the man's six-shooter, smelling of the barrel. No smell of powder smoke, only gun oil. He checked the cylinder . . . five bullets. Fully loaded, as most men let the hammer down on an empty chamber when riding across country. It was safer that way. He did it himself.

Well . . . no gunfight. The gun had not been fired and the man had not been expecting trouble, as the thong was still in place. His first action would have been to slip that free.

There was a bullet hole through the man's shirt near the heart. No blood around it to speak of, but that was often the case.

He looked again at the body, frowning a little. Disturbed, he studied it. What was bothering him?

The shirt . . . that was it. The shirt was too large for the man's neck. Of course, a man needing a shirt would buy what he could get . . . but there was a difference here. This man's clothes fitted to perfection . . . finely tooled black boots, the silver spurs polished, the black broadcloth pants fitted perfectly, and so did the fringed buckskin jacket, beautifully tanned to an almost white. This was a man who cared about his appearance, a neat, careful man, so why the too large shirt?

Well . . . There might have been many reasons and it was time he got back home. He started to slip the gun back into its holster, then glanced at it again.

It was a gun that had been much handled . . . The holster, too, was worn. Polished and in good shape, but worn. It was the gun and the holster of a man who knew how to use a gun, and who would have been good with it.

"Big Injun? What do you think?"

The Indian stood up. "He good man . . . strong man. He ride far, I think. No drink. No smell. No bottle. Face strong . . . clean."

Borden rubbed his jaw thoughtfully, studying the dead man again. Big Injun didn't like it and neither did he. Something was wrong here.

"Murder," Big Injun said. "This man . . . no know he would be shot. Sudden, I think."

Uneasily, Borden Chantry stared at the dusty floor. Damn it, was he going to have problems now? Why couldn't the dead man have been the drunken brawler he had expected?

Big Injun believed the man had been shot from ambush. Or, at least, shot when he did not expect it. Perhaps by someone he trusted . . . But in the street? Who? And the man was a stranger. Could someone have followed him?

It was a one-street town . . . one business street, at least, with a few side streets and back streets on which there were residences.

His small white house was rented from Hyatt Johnson, a square, four-room house with a white picket fence around it, a few feet of lawn, with some flowers carefully cultivated and watered by hand, and behind the house a small red barn and a corral.

Across the lane to the left there was a considerable pasture when he ran a dozen head of cattle and a few horses. Borden Chantry always kept a half-dozen horses, his best riding stock, in the corral at the barn.

He went down the lane and through the back gate. He could hear a faint rattle of dishes from the kitchen so we went up the steps.

"Oh, Borden! You're back!" Bess came to him quickly. Her eyes scanned his face. "Was it bad? Is everything all right?"

"He's in jail. I recovered the horses."

"Are you all right?" She held his arms, looking up into his face.

"Sure. It was nothing."

"Sit down. There's coffee, and I'll fix some eggs."

"I'll have the coffee, but I had breakfast with Lang. There's been some shooting down there. A man's been found dead in the street."

"Another one? Oh, Borden! I wish . . . I wish we could move back east. Anywhere. I don't want Tom growing up with all this shooting and killing. All this violence."

It was an old discussion, and he merely shrugged. "You married a rancher, Bess, and when I can get on my feet, I'll go back to ranching. This is my country and I belong here. As for being marshal . . . somebody has to do it."

"But why does it have to be you?" she protested.

"I am good with a gun, and they know it. More

than that, I know when not to use a gun, and they
know that, too."

The coffee tasted good, and it was pleasant here in
the kitchen. Bess moved about, doing the usual things
for breakfast, and he leaned back in his chair, still a
little tired from the long, hard ride.

The man had taken two horses and had swapped
saddles, that was what had fooled Kim Baca. He had
good horses and he stopped only long enough to switch
rigging, and so he had overtaken the horse thief before
he could get far. Baca had expected no pursuit to
catch him. That was half of it, of course, getting there
fast and unexpected.

"This is no ordinary killin', Bess. Leastwise it doesn't
look it. Nice lookin' young man, maybe about my age
or a mite older. Somebody shot him when he wasn't
expecting it. Laid for him, likely."

"Will you be gone all day?"

"Most of it." He finished his coffee and went into
the bedroom to change his shirt. His mind kept returning to the dead man. Of course, he could simply bury
him and that would be an end to it, but it wouldn't be
doing his job. Not doing it right. He'd been hired by
the city fathers and it was his job to keep the peace and
punish the evildoer . . . or hold them for judgment.

He frowned. The dead man had eaten at the Bon-
Ton, had paid for his meal and left. He should have
asked whether it was breakfast or dinner . . . or even
supper. Anyway, it would seem, the man had been
around town a few hours.

Well, what did he have? The victim had left the
Bon-Ton. The next morning he had been found dead
. . . So where had he been? Not that there were so
many places to go.

Chantry came out of the bedroom, stuffing his shirt
into his pants. Bess turned on him. "Borden? Where
did the man come from?"

"We don't know," he said. "That's something to find
out."

"And how did he get here?"

He glanced at her, grinning. "Now why didn't I

think of that? How *did* he get here? Pays to have a smart wife."

"It's just common sense, that's all. If he did not come by stage, he had to ride horseback."

He picked up his hat. "So where's his horse? I'd pin my badge on you if I could find a place to pin it."

She pushed him away. "You go find out how he got here. That will keep you out of mischief."

He closed the gate behind him thoughtfully. There was one stage in and one stage out each day. If the stranger had come by stage he had arrived sometime around midday, which meant he had been around town . . . a town with less than six hundred people . . . for several hours. Somebody had to have seen him.

Strolling along the dusty street Chantry reached the boardwalk, paused and stamped dust from his boots. A girl was walking toward him, a pretty girl with a lively face, big blue eyes and just a little overdressed and over-bangled.

"Lucy Marie?"

She paused, apprehensively. It was partly the badge, he suspected, and partly that he was known to be happily married.

"How's Mary Ann?"

"Ailing. She don't seem to get much better. I . . . I wish she could get away from here. She needs a rest."

"Tell her I asked about her."

Mary Ann Haley had lived in town for two years, occupying a house on a back street with Lucy Marie and a couple of others. Now she was ill . . . consumption, probably. A lot of the girls on the line seemed to pick it up.

Chantry returned to the barn and looked at the dead man on the table. He would have to be buried soon, yet the weather was cool to cold and they could wait a little while. Yet somehow he was reluctant to commit the man to the earth. Such a man must have a home . . . He kept himself too well to be just a drifter.

The door opened and Doc Terwilliger came in. "Is that the man?"

"It is. Look at him, Doc. There's something wrong. That man's mighty well dressed in frontier style. I

mean his clothes fit . . . he's had them made for him.
He's got a gun that's seen use. He's wearin' spurs that
look like Mexico or California, and most of the riders
around here these days are Kansas or Missouri boys
with a few drifters from Texas. He's been out in the
sun . . . you can see that. His gun ain't been fired lately
but it's cared for. Seems to me the only thing that
don't look right is that shirt. I can't see a man who
dresses as careful as him wearin' a shirt two sizes too
big."

Doc Terwilliger was forty-five, with twenty years of
it in army service, and there was little he had not
seen.

"I was just settin' here, Doc, wondering how you'd
get a shirt off a dead man who's prob'ly started to
stiffen up."

"Let's get the coat off first. He's not as stiff as you'd
expect. Here . . . lend a hand."

Lifting the dead man they worked his arms from
the sleeves and got the buckskin coat off. Doc ex-
amined it thoughtfully, then handed it to Borden Chantry.

He held the coat up. There was a little blood on the
back, but very little, considering the wound had been
in the front. And there was no bullet hole.

"I'll be damned!" he said. "Looks like the bullet
never got through."

"It did though," Doc said grimly. "Look here a
minute." With his surgical scissors he cut the shirt up
the back and they took it off. Doc tilted the body on
one side and they looked at it. Doc's face was grim.

"Shot twice," he said, "the first one in the back at
point-blank range. See? The power burns? And scattered grains of powder penetrated the skin.

"That shot was supposed to kill him, but it didn't.
See here? He was shot a second time, and from the
trajectory the killer was either lying on the floor shooting up or he was standing up as the supposedly dead
man started to rise off the floor. I'd say the latter."

"Only one bullet hole in the shirt," Borden said.
"Doc, d' you figure whoever it was shot this man, but
not wanting it to look like he was shot in the back, he

switched shirts, taking off the one the dead man had and substituting another that was too large? He was probably planning on shooting the dead man again, and then the victim started to sit up, and he shot him . . . killed him . . . although he would have died from the first shot.

"Then he put the man's coat on him and dropped the body where it would look like he was killed in a drunken fight."

Doc nodded. "That sounds right, Bord. This was deliberate, cold-blooded murder, the way I see it."

"I reckon so . . . I reckon so."

"What're you going to do, Bord?"

Chantry shrugged. "Doc, a killin' when both men are armed and responsible is one thing. Outright murder's another. I'm never going to quit until we get this man in jail."

"Bord, think of what you're facing. We've only a few hundred people in town, but there's over a hundred miners and prospectors around, and probably fifty or sixty cowboys and drifters. Why, the man who did this is long gone."

"No," Borden Chantry spoke slowly. "I don't think so, Doc. No drifter would have bothered to cover it up like this. He'd just have run. He'd have got him a horse and pulled his stakes.

"This here is murder, all right, an' I'm bettin' the man who done it is still around!"

"Then be careful, Bord. Be very careful. When the murderer realizes you suspect somebody local, your number's up. He'll be running scared, Bord, and his only way out will be to kill you!"

Chapter II

Borden Chantry, at twenty-four, had been doing a man's work since he was eleven. To shirk a job or sidestep a responsibility had never occurred to him, for in the life around there was no place for such things. A man was judged on how he did his work, not on what he had or where he came from. At eleven he had been riding herd on a bunch of cattle owned by a neighbor who had gone to Texas, and he took his payment in calves.

By the time he was sixteen he had thirty-two head wearing his own brand, and had sold about the same number. That was the year he rode to Texas to help bring a herd back to Colorado.

He had survived a brush with Comanches near Horse Head Crossing on the Pecos. At seventeen he had followed some horses stolen by the Kiowa and stole them back, along with all the mounts the Kiowas themselves had, setting them afoot.

Most of the time it was hard, brutal work, which he never considered either hard or brutal. It was simply his job, and he did it. From the time he was eleven until he was twenty-three, he could not recall a sunrise that did not find him in the saddle—nor a sunset, for that matter.

He grew tall and lean. He learned to read sign like an Apache and to use a gun. He was considered a top hand, not the best puncher around, but certainly up there among them.

When the town council made him marshal he was broke, still owning a wide spread of land, but nearly all his cattle were gone, and some of his horses. To keep his family alive meant moving to town and finding work.

As marshal his job was to enforce the law, and to him the laws were the rules that made civilization work. Without them there was chaos. They were not a

15

restriction upon his freedom, but the doorway to greater freedom, for they established certain rules that men were not to transgress. In the land in which he had grown up it was customary to settle disputes with a gun. Consequently men, unless drunk, were cautious with their language and respectful of one another.

Murder was rare, although it did happen, and now he had a murder on his hands. Worst of all, he had no skills that would make easy the solving of such a crime. He was simply a common-sense sort of man who knew only one way, and he started coping with murder as he started anything else . . . one point at a time.

Who was the dead man? Identification was important, for then one might learn who might want him eliminated. Also, what was he doing in town? Where had he come from?

Bess had put her finger on his starting point: How did the man get here?

The stage office was open when Chantry arrived there, and he pushed the door open. The office was simply a counter across the room that cut off one third of it. Behind that was a desk, a swivel chair, and some filing cabinets, all much battered, all but the chair stacked with papers.

George Blazer, with a green eyeshade and sleeve garters, was at the desk.

"Howdy, Bord? Hear you got you a dead one!"

"He's dead all right . . . Murdered."

"Murdered?" George was startled. "Are you sure?"

"You recall a man coming in on the stage the last coupla days? Tall man, black hair. Nice lookin' feller, wore a fringed buckskin coat with some Indian beadwork. Black broadcloth pants?"

"No, nobody like that, Bord. Travel's been light the last few days. Hyatt was over to Denver, but he got in three, four days ago. No, I can surely say, no such man come in by stage."

"Did you see him around?"

"Oh, sure! Three or four times. He was havin' a drink down to the Corral when I first saw him. He was alone then, I did notice he seemed interested in

folks along the street. I mean he was watching them
. . . Women, mostly."

"Well, that's normal. Did he talk to anybody? See
him with anybody at all?"

"Nope. Sure didn't. I saw him there at the saloon,
and walking across the street several times, or up and
down the street."

"Ever see him ridin'?"

"No, come to think of it, I didn't. It was yesterday
I saw him around. I'm out front a good deal, shifting
trunks around, or loading mail sacks on the stage, or
just takin' the air. That's how I seen him."

Borden Chantry walked out front and leaned
against the awning post. Some drunk might have pot-
shotted an innocent stranger, although that was unlikely. But when somebody went to the trouble to
murder a man and hide it . . . Well, there had to be a
reason.

He took off his hat and wiped the sweatband. To
think that even now the murderer might be watching
him, wondering what he was thinking, gave him an
eerie feeling. He was uneasy, not liking not knowing
who his enemy might be. Always before, he had
known. Indians, rustlers, horse thieves . . . They were
tangible, and he knew how to cope with them. A murderer, who might be watching his every move, ready
to try killing him if he got too close . . . well, that was
something different.

He strolled about town, putting the question here
and there. Several people remembered the man, nobody remembered anything in particular about him.

If he rode a horse he left it somewhere. Borden
walked into the shadowed livery stable, a wide door at
each end. It smelled of fresh hay, fresh manure, and
harness leather. He walked down the wide aisle between the stalls, looking at the horses.

Lang's big black was there. It rolled its eyes at him
as he passed. And there were Hyatt's matched bays
which he drove to a buckboard. Hyatt rode astride
from time to time, but preferred the buckboard.

There were no strange horses in the barn.

As he returned to the front entrance, Ab came from his tack room which was also his sleeping quarters. "Somethin' fur ya, Marshal?"

"Checkin' the horses. Did a tall man in a fringed buckskin coat come in here?"

"Nope . . . No strangers this week 'ceptin' that drummer who was in here from Kansas City. He was sellin' hair oil an' such. Some ladies' fixin's. Nope, nobody."

In a small town, people noticed strangers. In a small western town, they noticed horses. Yet few people seemed to have seen this man, and nobody had seen him with a horse. At least nobody Chantry had found.

It was likely the man had come in before daylight or after dusk . . . maybe at suppertime when nobody much was on the street. But if he came in at dusk he had to stay somewhere. Borden crossed the street to the hotel.

The lobby was small with a desk at one side, an old cracked leather settee, two huge leather chairs, and another chair made entirely, except for the seat, of longhorn horns. On the walls there were several heads of antelope, deer, and buffalo, including at the back of the desk a longhorn steer head with nine-foot horns.

Elsie Carter was behind the desk, as she was most of the time.

"Yes, he was in. Asked me if I had a room for the night, and I told him I had. He said he'd be back for it."

"Did he give you his name?"

"No, he didn't. No name. I will say he was a right handsome man, however. Right handsome . . . Had a familiar look, too."

"Familiar? Like somebody around here?"

"No . . . no, but like somebody I've seen. Been bothering me ever since he was in. He was like, yet not like. I dunno."

"Elsie, you've been around towns like this since you was a kid, and in the hotel business most of the time. You've got a knowing way about folks. What would you say about him? Anything at all. I just got nothing to tie to."

She touched a hand to her hair, then leaned a fat

elbow on the counter. "Marshal, I can tell you one thing. That man *was* somebody. He had the manner, the style. I tell you something else. He was a man who was good with a gun. They got a way about them, Marshal. You got it yourself. You can tell it in a man . . . No swagger, no show-off, just a sort of assurance, confidence . . . I don't know. But he had it."

"You think he was gunnin' for somebody?"

"No. He was looking for somebody, but not that way. I could tell the way he turned when somebody came in, and the way he looked when somebody went down the street. But he had that rawhide thong over his gun hammer and he never taken it off. Minute he walked in I spotted him, and I looked at that thong. You reckon he was a marshal hisself?"

"I don't know, Elsie, I surely don't."

Borden walked out on the street. "Hell of a marshal you make!" he said, half-aloud, and with disgust. "A man rides into a town and you can't even find his horse!"

Think back. If a man rode into town, what would he be coming for? To buy land? To buy cattle? Land wasn't moving much these days and it was the wrong time for cattle-buying.

Irritably, Chantry stared down the street. He should have taken the advice he got and just buried the man like any victim of a shooting, but he had to open it up, make a big thing of it. It was nigh on to noontime already, and all his questions had led to nothing he hadn't known or guessed. He still did not know who the man was, where he came from or why he came to town.

He started down the street and suddenly a boy darted from an alleyway. "Hi, Marshal!" It was Billy McCoy. That kid was everywhere, into everything.

"Hey, Billy!"

The boy came back with a retort. "Yeah, Marshal? You want I should ketch a rustler for you?"

"You leave that to me for a coupla years, Billy. What I want to know is did you see the dead man around town? You know, that—"

"Aw, sure! I seen him. I snuck into the barn over

there and looked at him . . . First dead man I ever seen up close."

"You stay out of there, Billy. That man's not on display. What I mean is, did you see him before? When he was alive?"

"Sure, I saw him. I saw him when he first came into town . . . It wasn't quite daybreak yet. Pa, he woke me up when he came in and I got up to get a drink from the well.

"I seen that man come ridin' in. Ridin' a mighty fine sorrel horse with three white stockings. Prettiest horse I seen this year, and a good walker, too. Why, that horse could walk as fast as most horses trot."

"Where did he go? Where did he leave his horse?"

"How should I know? I went back an' tried to get to sleep. He was ridin' right up Main Street when I seen him. But I never seen the horse again. I saw the man two, three times. I saw him around town durin' the day, an' I saw him that night when he was drunk."

"Drunk, did you say?"

"Well, he looked it. He come up the street and kind of fell against the building. He shaken his head a couple of times and started on up the street. He was weavin' around some . . . kind of like he was drunk, but . . . he might have been sick, Marshal. He just might have been sick."

"Thanks, Billy," Chantry said, and continued on down the street.

Big Injun was waiting at the barn. "You give me dollar, I dig grave."

"All right, Big Injun. You do that. Dig it deep, now." He turned away when a thought came to him. "Big Injun, this man came into town riding a tall sorrel, three white stockings. Did you see it?"

Big Injun got a shovel from a corner of the barn and walked back to the door. "Tall horse? Seventeen hands?"

"Could be."

"Me see 'um. Go north."

North . . . ? Borden Chantry paused there and considered. The man had come into town riding a mighty fine horse . . . yet where was the horse? The man was dead. His horse had to be somewhere around.

Chantry glanced left and right. He could see Johnny McCoy, Billy's father, sitting on the end of the board-walk near the Corral.

Chantry suddenly realized the one place he had not asked questions about a murder was the most likely place to start—Time Reardon's Corral Saloon. The victim, it had been said, had been drunk.

Reardon, a small man with neatly combed hair and sly, careful eyes stood behind his bar. "How are you, Marshal? What's on your mind?"

"There's been a murder. Tall man, buckskin coat. Have you seen him?"

"He was in here. Had one drink, then left."

"I heard he was drunk."

"Drunk? Him? I doubt it, but if he was he didn't get it here."

"You said you doubted he was drunk . . . Why?"

Reardon took a cigar from a box, clipped the end and lighted it. "Wasn't the type. I've been in this busi-ness a long time, Marshal, and that man was no drink-er. A drink . . . yes. But drunk? I doubt it."

"Did you know him?"

Reardon hesitated . . . a moment too long. "No, no I did not know him. But I'll tell you two things about him, Marshal." He smiled thinly, no smile in his eyes. "You know I always like to help the law. I'll tell you two things. Whoever he was, he wasn't running from anything, and he wasn't hunting anybody. He was a man I'd lay odds on in a gun battle, and he was carry-ing money."

"Money?"

"He was careful, Marshal, but I saw it. He had a small sack hung inside his waistband on the left side. It had to be gold."

"He had only one drink?"

"That's all. Paid for it with a quarter . . . You know my drinks are two for a quarter." Reardon puffed slowly on his cigar. "I called after him, told him he had an-other coming and he said to forget it, or give it to somebody who needed it more than he did."

"When I asked if you'd seen him before, you hesitated."

"Did I? Well, maybe I did. Let me put it this way, Marshal. I had never seen *that* man before, but once I knew somebody who looked very much like him, and if they are related let me suggest you find the killer and find him fast."

"What's that mean?"

"It means that *if* that man should be part of the family I am talking about, you have the killer in jail before they come looking. If you don't they'll take the town apart, plank by plank, brick by brick."

"I don't think we'd let them do it," Chantry said gently. "There's some pretty salty boys in this town."

"Yes, there are." Reardon dusted ash from his cigar. "Marshal, people have said some pretty hard things about me, but I don't think you ever heard anybody question my nerve."

"That's right," Chantry agreed, honestly. "I never did."

"Then understand this. I have a business here, a fair-sized investment in the town, but if those boys come looking I am going to crawl into the nearest hole and pull the hole in after me."

"Who are they?"

"I've said enough, and I pray to the good Lord that I am wrong, but Marshal . . . find your killer, and find him quick."

Chantry thanked Reardon and left.

What he needed now was a chance to sit down, to think a little. Despite himself, Reardon's remarks had worried him. That was all he would need, a bunch of hard-nosed riders coming in looking for a murderer. He'd seen such crowds before, and had seen some of the shootings that resulted. Usually the town won, but men died and property was damaged, and it was not the sort of thing he wanted to happen.

At the Bon-Ton he took a pot of coffee and a cup and went to a seat by the window. He sat down, filled his cup, and leaned back in his chair. All he still had was a tall dead man who had ridden a sorrel horse with three white stockings.

A man suspected of being a dangerous man to tackle, a man who did not seem like a drinker yet had been drunk . . . or apparently so.

At least, he had something to start with. If he could just find that horse!

Forty years ago this had been Kiowa country and then the buffalo hunters had come. There was a good spring here, so some of the hide-hunters had camped nearby. And later some suppliers had come in and opened a trading post for the hunters, building the place out of the board-stiff, iron-hard hides.

Within a few months a stage stop had been added to the trading post and saloon and the cluster of dug-outs and hide-shelters. One of the buffalo hunters squatted on a waterhole a few miles south and brought in some cattle. Then some copper ore had been found and a small mine started working. So the town had come into being.

Hyatt Johnson's father had been one of the original buffalo hunters. George Riggins, the old marshal, had been another.

The door opened and Lang Adams came in. Seeing Borden, he came around to his table. "Well? How's the crime detection business?"

"Slow," Borden replied irritably. "Have some coffee."

"You worry too much." Lang filled his cup. "After all it's only a job."

"Yeah," Chantry replied shortly, "but it may mean my scalp. It may mean the town."

Lang looked at him sharply. "The town? What does that mean?"

Chantry repeated what Reardon had said, and in reply to a question, added, "That's all I know, but you and I both know there's some outfits around that are as loyal to one another as some of the Scottish clans. You step on one of their toes and they all holler. Well, it looks like somebody stepped on a toe."

"I wouldn't worry about it. It's unlikely anybody will ever know what happened to him, and probably nobody cares."

"I care. It happened in my town."

"You take it too seriously," Lang said. "Look, the man is dead. More than likely he deserved shooting. I know how you feel, but what are you going to gain? You won't get paid a dollar more, and if anybody does come looking, just say you don't know anything about it.

"The man was a stranger. It is likely that if he was murdered it was by somebody who followed him here, somebody who may have come just for that reason. And when it was done, he simply left."

"Maybe . . . And again, maybe not. One thing I do know, Lang. If he's still around here, I am going to find him. And when I find him, he will go to jail . . . Or hang."

Chapter III

Borden Chantry was a puzzled man. He wanted very much to do his job right, but he had never been any hand at puzzles . . . Trails, yes. He could work out a trail, and sometimes that took some doing. Well, why not work this out the same way? The idea gave him confidence.

Time Reardon had said the stranger had been carrying a well-filled poke . . . So where was it? Time had noticed it, and it was likely that others had. Suddenly Borden was aware he had seen nothing of Puggsey Kerns or Frank Hurley, two of Reardon's associates.

To say they were thugs was understating the case. George Riggins had both men in jail from time to time but had been able to prove nothing that would permit keeping them there. If a drunk was robbed in the vicinity the chances were one or both had a hand in it, and it was likely they had been involved in some stage hold-ups out of Cheyenne, but there was no evidence.

So far they had not been seen on the street this morning, but it was early.

With nothing else to do Chantry strolled back to the barn. Again he looked at the body, and for the first time checked something he had observed on his first sight of the body without having it really register. The dead man's knuckles were lightly skinned.

Had he hit somebody? It looked like it. The dead man had solid, well-made hands.

No marks on his face. The fight, if there had been a fight, had been a one-sided affair.

He unstrapped the dead man's gun, went through his pockets again . . . Nothing.

The buckskin jacket was well-made . . . Indian-made, and Cheyenne by the style. Now the Cheyenne were a Plains people although they were found sometimes far down into Texas and over against the Rockies in Colorado. The jacket was nicely kept but was not new which gave Chantry the feeling this man had lived or traveled in Cheyenne country and probably was friendly with them, Otherwise to get a jacket like this he'd have had to trade a pony at least, or a good rifle.

The Cheyenne jacket and the spurs . . . well, that was a hint. This rider probably had been in the Rocky Mountain country of Colorado or northern New Mexico or both . . . Two to three days ride from here . . . Maybe longer, depending on his horse and his ambition.

"Big Injun," Chantry suggested, "you make him a coffin . . . All right?"

"Blanket good enough." Big Injun was abrupt. "Worms eat him, anyway."

"I want a coffin for him. Will you make it or do I hire somebody else?"

"One dollar?"

"All right."

Everything with Big Injun was one dollar. Didn't he know what twenty-five cents was? Or was he smart enough not to learn?

Reardon had said the dead man had not had more than one drink, and had left immediately. So he had not gambled.

Street by street Chantry walked the town, checking every stable and corral. No sorrel horse with three white stockings . . . no strange horse of any kind. The last stable he checked was Johnny McCoy's.

Billy McCoy was standing in the yard spinning a rope, trying to make a circle he could jump in and out of, but not having much luck.

"Howdy, Marshal! You still huntin' after that dead man's horse?"

"Sure am. You recall what brand he wore?"

Billy stopped spinning his rope and scowled, thoughtfully. "No, sir. I surely don't. Guess I didn't even see it."

Chantry looked at Billy again. A western man or boy just naturally looks at brands . . . he *always* looks at them. Could Billy be lying? And if so, why?

"Mind if I look in your barn? I'm checking every-one."

"Go ahead. There's no horses in there. Ours are in the corral."

The small barn was shadowed and still. There was no horse there, only a few odds and ends of old harness, a few coils of rope, some old, worn-down boots, long unused, and the usual tools.

There was some manure at one of the stalls, and Chantry paused, glancing at it again.

Johnny McCoy kept his barn clean . . . or Billy did. About once a week it was cleaned out and fresh straw was scattered on the dirt floor. There was manure at only one of the makeshift stalls, but what made Borden Chantry take that second look was the position of it. Either that manure had been dropped by a big horse or one that had pulled back to the end of its tether be-fore dropping it.

Taking off his hat Chantry wiped the sweatband. It had become a habit when he was thinking . . . if what he was doing could be called thinking, he reflected irritably.

Looking carefully around, he checked everything, and everything seemed to be right. Yet the manure worried him. There might have been a lot of reasons for its position that were perfectly natural, but it also might have been left by a tall, long-barreled horse . . . say one that was seventeen hands high.

Opening the door a little wider for more light he walked back to the stall and studied it. At a rough place in the boards on the right-hand side he found a few sorrel hairs. Yet . . . . it meant nothing. There might have been a dozen sorrel horses in that stall at one time or another.

He started for the door when something caught his eye. Among the several ropes hung from nails . . . three on one nail in one place . . . was one . . . He lifted a couple of grass ropes and beneath it hung a rawhide riata, and a long one.

He heard a slight movement and turned to see Billy staring at him. "Billy?" he spoke gently. "Where'd this rope come from?"

"I dunno. One o' Pa's I guess."

"Now, Billy, you know your pa never used a raw-hide rope in his life. I've punched cows with him . . . and a better puncher never walked . . . but I never saw him with a rawhide riata."

"Well . . . I found it."

"Found it where?"

"Yonder." He indicated a gap in the brush some distance off. "I figured . . . well . . . if nobody come huntin' I'd . . . well, I'd sort of keep it."

"That's logical, Billy. But that's a mighty fine rope and somebody would surely miss it. I wish you'd brought it to me first, then if nobody showed up wanting it, it would be yours."

"Sure enough?" He glanced enviously at the rope. "I never seen one that long."

"That's a Mexican rope, Billy, or one used by the Californios. They use rawhide riatas . . . I've seen them braiding them. You come by the house someday and I'll show you how it's done."

He squatted on his heels. "Billy, I think that riata belonged to the murdered man. Would you have any ideas about that?"

"No, sir. I reckon not."

"That sorrel, Billy? Was he ever in this barn?"

"No, sir. Not that I know of." Suddenly Billy's eyes became fearful. "You . . . you ain't thinkin' Pa done it?"

"No, Billy, I am not. I don't have any idea what was done or who did it. Your pa's a good man, Billy. He has his problems, like we all do, but he's no murderer. He might shoot a man in a stand-up fight but he'd never back-shoot him."

Borden Chantry got to his feet. "Billy, I've got to find that horse. The first thing I have to do is find that horse and get the brand . . . I've had a hint, Billy, that the man may have belonged to a very tough outfit, and if they find he has been murdered they may come shootin'. If that happens a lot of your good friends may get hurt, so I've got to find the killer . . . fast."

"Yes, sir. You think that horse was in our barn?"

"I don't know, Billy. When was the last time you were in there? The barn, I mean?"

"I dunno. Maybe the day before yesterday. Ain't much call to go in, and I been exercisin' Hyatt Johnson's horses. He gives me fifty cents a week to take 'em out an' ride 'em around so they don't get too frisky for him."

"Then a horse might have been here without you knowin'?"

"Well . . . maybe. But who'd put one in there without askin'?"

"Nobody I can think of. Billy, where's your pa?"

"He's inside. He's asleep."

"When he wakes up, you tell him I wish he'd come down to the office. I want to talk to him a little bit."

He walked slowly back up the street to the boardwalk, then along the street. Only a few rigs and a half dozen horses were tied along the street. How could a man ride into such a town, get himself murdered and then have his horse disappear?

Lang was right. He was wasting his time. He'd be far better off hunting turkeys out at the ranch. At least, he'd have something to show for it.

Chantry went to his own home and saddled his Appaloosa. He tried to rotate his horses to keep them all in shape, and it was the Appaloosa's turn, although he suspected this would be a short ride.

He found the place where Billy said he had picked up the riata . . . Sure enough, the tracks of a big horse with a long, beautiful stride.

For an hour he followed a winding trail through the brush, skirting the town rather than riding away from it, and taking a devious route. Suddenly the rider had come out into a lane, and Chantry swore softly.

The trail was gone! Wiped out in cow tracks.

He drew up, pushed his hat back on his head and studied the situation. This was another indication that the murderer, if it was indeed the man who was riding the sorrel, had been familiar with the town and its people. For he had come toward this spot, knowing that it was along this lane Old Man Peterson drove his

dairy herd, the herd that supplied milk and butter to
the town.

Each morning and each evening that herd went
along this lane, successfully wiping out any tracks that
might have been left.

Yet this again made Chantry puzzled. Whoever had
done it had gambled the tracker would quit here, or
had not known how a good tracker works . . . a mistake Johnny McCoy would not be likely to make.

For Borden Chantry simply rode out of the lane
where the cattle had traveled and rode as closely paral-
lel to it as possible, owing to the crowding brush. Unless the rider of the sorrel was going into Peterson's
home corral he had to turn off somewhere. And on the
other side there were barns, corrals, the backs of yards
belonging to people of the town.

Taking his time, studying the ground as he rode,
Borden Chantry worked his way in and around the
brush until suddenly he saw the tracks where the sorrel had turned off. Riding through thick brush he had
even left a few hairs on the stiff branches of the brush.
A little bored by the obviousness of it, Chantry fell
in behind and followed the trail at a canter . . . It
dipped into a dry wash, up the other side after a hundred yards or so, then through a scattered forest of
juniper and up to shelving rock where the rider held
to the rock as much as possible.

Obviously he was trying to leave no trail, but Chantry held his pace. The white hoof scars made by iron
shoes upon the rock were obvious enough. Suddenly he
lost the trail, swung in a wide circle and picked it up
again.

The trail merged with another, made by a track that
looked familiar, then they separated . . . The first track
was older. Since the last shower, but older.

And then, as if lifted upon a magic carpet, the trail
of the sorrel disappeared!

No tracks . . . nothing.

A wide circle left and another right . . . still nothing.
He retraced his steps to where he had lost the trail.
There was a place where the horse had stood, had
moved about a bit, then vanished.

Stepping down from the saddle and standing beside his horse, he studied the ground. The wind was cool, stirring his hair at the forehead. He brushed the hair back and looked back toward town, only a few miles away, but out of sight.

There was a faint smell of dust and crushed cedar. How did he ever get himself into this fix, anyway?

What had somebody said? If he started getting too close he might get shot himself. And the worst of it was, he had no idea who would be shooting at him.

His thoughts suddenly reverted to Kim Baca, the horse thief he had gone after. At least, you knew where you stood with horse thieves . . . Which brought up another idea. What was Kim Baca doing in this area, anyway? It was out of his bailiwick entirely.

That was something he should ask about . . . just out of curiosity, and the answer might give him some further clue as to how the outlaw mind operated.

He studied the ground again. Now what could have happened here? There were no magic carpets in eastern Colorado in this day and time. Nor did horses disappear into thin air.

Yet this horse had vanished . . . how had it vanished? If it left this place it had to walk. Nobody could fly it out, nobody could carry it. He saw no brush marks, as if a trail had been brushed away . . . something always pretty obvious but sometimes attempted.

There was no sense moving on. Sometimes a man can just wear himself out moving around when he is just a sight better off to stay put and ponder. That was how he came to see that thread. It wasn't more than an inch or two long and it was hung up under a prickly pear, but it was a thread from a tow sack. What some folks call burlap. Then it was, plain as shootin'.

Whoever had been riding that horse had gotten down and wrapped its hooves in burlap.

Now that horse wasn't going to go far with those contraptions on its feet, and it didn't.

About a quarter of a mile further he found a place where the arroyo bank had caved, and as he pulled up on the Appaloosa a coyote went slinking away down the canyon.

There below him was a heap of rock and dirt that had fallen from the rim some ten feet above. It had either caved or been caved.

Leaving his horse standing, Chantry dug in his heels and went down the slide. Pulling loose a large rock he toppled it off to one side, then scraped at the dirt. As the dirt came away a bit of sorrel hide was revealed.

It took the better part of an hour to get enough dirt moved, what with more caving, and to get at the horse's side, then to uncover it to look for the brand.

It was gone.

The brand had been cut away in a neat circle, taking off a piece of hide about eight or nine inches in diameter.

The brand was gone, and with it all chance of identifying either horse or man.

Borden Chantry swore softly, bitterly. Then he started to rise and one leg cramped and he staggered. It was all that saved him.

He felt the sharp *whip* of the bullet as it passed!

Chapter IV

Borden Chantry was a quiet, easygoing but serious-minded man who had known little but hard work most of his life and expected nothing to be that easy. Although an expert with both pistol and rifle, he had never felt the necessity of proving it to any man, and the few fights he had were with fists. A man with a quiet sense of humor and laugh wrinkles at the corners of his eyes, he was not amused now.

That bullet had come too close, and whoever fired was shooting for the money.

His reaction was instinctive and correct. He threw himself down, and rolled over into the shelter of the opposite bank of the arroyo.

His horse was on the bank some thirty yards away and across the arroyo, and he was of no mind to try getting to his horse with a rifleman waiting for him to do just that.

Working his way swiftly along the bank he came to a place where the bank curved sharply west, which was in the direction from which the would-be killer had fired.

He rounded the curve, rifle up and ready for a shot from the hip, and when the wash was empty before him he scrambled up a notch where additional water had trickled down, and lying there, he listened.

Nothing.

He had ridden over this area several times in rounding up strays and knew that some dozen yards from where he now lay there was a nest of brush and boulders. It would be a perfect spot from which to survey the area, but it might be the spot where the killer waited.

He considered that. Normally a cautious man, anger made him aggressive, and he did not like lying still, waiting for another shot. His were the instincts of the hunter, and for the moment hunting was what he was paid for. So he came out of the notch at a run and sprinted for the nest of boulders. A rifle barked somewhere off to his left but the shot came late and too far back, and the next instant he was into the rocks and getting lined up for a shot.

Then he heard the drum of horse's hooves, and slowly he relaxed. Undoubtedly the unknown marksman was getting away, so let him go. Yet Borden Chantry waited. He hunched down in a good spot where he could see all around him and where he had his horse in his field of vision.

He waited a slow half hour, then got up and walked slowly off in the direction from which the shots had come. The air was cool . . . coming on to rain.

A half hour's scouting brought him nothing. Yet the man's horse had to have been tied somewhere, and reluctantly Borden gave up the search and crossed the arroyo to get his own horse. Mounting, he rode back and searched again.

No luck. With more time, maybe.

He turned his horse toward home, stripped the gear and turned it into the corral.

Kim Baca was a slender, wiry young man, half-Irish, the other half Spanish and Apache. No more than twenty-two, he was already a known man in four states, two territories and Mexico. He had a lean, saturnine face, a quizzical sense of humor, and was known to be a dead shot, yet he had never been involved in any shooting scrapes.

Borden Chantry picked up his keys and walked back to the cell. Over his shoulder he called, "Big Injun? Bring us a pot of coffee and a couple of cups."

He opened the cell and stepped in, leaving the door ajar for Big Injun.

Kim Baca looked up at him, smiling faintly. "Aren't you scared I'll get away?"

Chantry grinned and shrugged. "Go ahead . . . if you feel lucky."

Baca laughed. "Not me. The odds are all wrong.

Besides, I saw you in a couple of fights. You're no bargain."

"Thanks." Chantry tilted his chair back against the wall. "Kim, what in God's name made you pull a fool thing like lifting Johnson's horses? Everybody in the country knows that team."

"How was I to know that? Anyway, I was mad. Somebody beat me to the horse I was after."

Was it a hunch? Or had he guessed it before this? Chantry looked up at him. "Big sorrel? Three white stockings?"

Baca stared at him, then took the toothpick on which he was chewing and threw it to the floor. "You mean you had me pegged? You even knew what horse I was after?"

"Mighty fine horse," Chantry replied, admitting nothing. "I wouldn't blame you."

Baca got up. "Marshal, you just don't know! That was one of the fastest-stepping horses I ever saw! Gentle as a baby, yet it could go all day an' all night! I tell you, I could have loved that horse! I mean it! I never wanted anything so bad in my life!"

"Know who owned it?"

"Hell, no! I picked him up in Raton Pass. I saw that horse coming and figured it might be the law on my tail, so I put my glass on him. You never saw a horse move like that one! I just told myself, 'Kim, this is it. That's your horse.' So I fell in behind him.

"I had to watch my step, too, because that rider, whoever he was, was canny. I hadn't been followin' him more'n a few miles before he knew it. Somehow or other he gave me the slip and I lost him until I rode into Trinidad and saw the horse tied to a hitching rail there."

"Remember the brand?" Chantry spoke casually, yet he was mentally holding his breath.

Did Baca hesitate? "No," he said, "I can't say that I do."

"You see any more of him?"

"No." Was there another instant of hesitation? "I heard him ask after this town, so I came on ahead.

Rode in here an' waited for him to make it . . . Then
he never showed."

"You never saw him again?"

"Marshal," Kim Baca spoke slowly, "I got a thing
about horses. I wouldn't admit to a thing in court an'
if you say I said this, I'll say I never . . . But I never
stole a horse to sell. I stole 'em because I wanted 'em. I
wanted 'em my own self. Except that team of Johnson's. I never figured to steal them horses, just got
mad an' stole 'em out of spite when I didn't get the
sorrel."

Borden Chantry filled Kim's cup and his own. He
had an idea what was in Kim's mind. He was a known
horse thief, caught with the goods. In many places that
would have meant an immediate hanging, yet Chantry
had arrested him, brought him back and was holding
him in jail.

A man had been murdered. That man's horse had
disappeared. What more likely suspect than Kim Baca?
What easier way to close the books on a crime?

"Baca," he said slowly, "you punched a lot of cows
in your time. You had the name of being a top hand.
Now you're in trouble. We *can* send you to the pen,
and you wouldn't cotton to that any more than me.

"Back yonder when I nabbed you, I could have
shot you and nobody would have cared or even asked
how come. I didn't. I took you in without a fight."

"You was slick. I got to admit it. And I was too
damn sure of myself."

"Well, whatever. Thing is you know I'll play square
if there's a way I can do it, and I'm not against givin'
you a break if you come clean. You know a good deal
more than you've said. You tell me and I'll try to talk
Johnson out of pressing charges."

Kim stared into his coffee cup, and Chantry felt
sympathy for the man. Right now Baca was trying to
study out how much he could trust Chantry.

"All right . . . You've been square. Trouble is I
don't know much . . . Only that somebody stole that
sorrel before I could. Right from under my nose."

"Did you see it done?"

"No, I never."

"Do you know who did it?"

That hesitation again. "No . . . no, I don't." Kim put down his cup. "Look, Marshal. I stood around the street watchin' for that horse 'n rider. They never showed . . . and then I saw the rider.

"So where's the horse? I studied on that, an' knowin' which way the man would come into town, I started studyin' on places that horse might be. I pegged it for one of two places. Either that stable with the corral and the two-room shack over east or Mary Ann Haley's."

The shack over east would be Johnny McCoy's . . . but why Mary Ann's?

He asked the question, and Baca shrugged. "He went there . . . that rider did. He went mighty early in the morning when they aren't receivin' guests as a rule, only they let him right in.

"I figured they knew him, the way they opened up for him, so I checked their stable. No horses but their driving horses for their rig. So then I went to the other place . . . That horse was sure enough there, but I heard stirrin' around inside and I took myself away from there."

"And then?"

"I come back that night, real late . . . and I seen a man ridin' off on that sorrel, slippin' off mighty quiet-like. I know a thief when I see one, and that man was a thief."

"Would you know him if you saw him?"

"N . . . no. No, I don't think so. He was kind of humped over in the saddle so's you couldn't make out his height."

Borden Chantry opened the cell door and stepped out, closing it after him. "Take your time with the coffee, Baca, and give it a thought. You're a good man on a trail. You help me, and I'll help you."

He went into the street and stood there, pulling his hat brim down against the glare. A wagon was coming slowly up the street and Johnson's dog got up lazily and moved out of the way.

Well, what did that get him? That Mary Ann Haley had seen the dead man. Had welcomed him . . . or somebody had . . . like a friend.

He shook his head. That didn't jell with what he already knew or surmised about the victim . . . What business could he have with a woman like Mary Ann? That early in the morning when they weren't in the habit of receiving guests?

He tried to add it all up, and came to nothing. "You're not much of a detective, Borden," he told himself.

A stranger had ridden into town with a poke of money, gold, probably. The following morning he was dead . . . murdered. His horse had been taken out and killed . . . the brand cut away.

Two things he knew—or was sure of in his own mind: The murderer was a local man, and he had not wanted the victim identified.

Which made the brand all-important.

He turned to start down the street and came face to face with Frank Hurley.

Hurley made as if to turn away but Chantry saw him in time. "Frank!"

Grudgingly, the man stopped. He was a lean, hard-visaged man who now carried a badly swollen eye, a split lip, and a swollen ear.

"You look like you tangled with a buzz saw," Chantry said, "or somebody with a bunch of knuckles."

"You want to see me about somethin'? If you do, say so, or I'm goin' down the street."

Chantry smiled. "Frank, if you take a step before I tell you to, I'll throw you in jail for loitering. Now you tell me. Who gave you the eye?"

"None of your damn business!"

"Where's Puggsey?"

"Up at the shack, I reckon. He minds his affairs, I mind mine."

"Tell me about it, Frank. If the story sounds good I may not arrest you for murder."

Frank Hurley's skin tightened. He glanced quickly, right and left. "Now see here, Marshal, that kind of talk can get a man hung. I never murdered nobody. Nobody, d' you hear?"

"The dead man had skinned knuckles. You have

been hit, obviously. I could build a case out of that, Frank."

"I never done nothing. You lay off . . . lay off, d' you hear? Time Reardon says—"

"You can tell Time for me that unless you boys tell me what you know I may throw all three of you in jail. You've all had it coming for a long time. The murdered man was in Time's place, there's evidence you were in a brawl and so was he . . . and I haven't heard of a fight all week. You think about it, Frank. Then if you're in a mind to talk, come around."

He went home for dinner.

At the table he told his wife about the case, reviewing it as much for himself as for her. "I got to talk to Mary Ann," he said, at last.

Bess stiffened. "Is that necessary, Borden? Is it really? What could that woman know? Of course, the man went there, but isn't it rather obvious?"

"Not at that hour."

He sat long over dinner, staring out at the sunlit street. It was a whole lot simpler out there on the range herding cows, branding stock, or doping the stock for screwworms. He could chase down a horse thief or throw a drunk in jail or take a gun off somebody, but figuring out a murder? He shook his head.

The one thing he had not mentioned to Bess was the shot taken at him. No use to worry her. She disliked the job in its every aspect, but what would they do otherwise? Money was scarce . . . What had become of the stranger's money?

Talking to Frank Hurley had been just a straw thrown into the wind. He knew pretty much what had happened that night, and although he could prove none of it, he could have written a report on it with what he knew was true.

"I'd lay a bet," he told Bess, "that Frank an' Puggsey followed that stranger into a dark street somewhere, an' jumped him. Only that stranger knew how to take care of himself and whipped 'em both, whipped 'em good.

"Only I'd like to know where the stranger was going and where he was coming from. I think Time will have them tell me. He's no fool."

Any man who would kill a horse like that wasn't worth shooting. So why had he killed it? Why not just take it out and turn it loose to go home?

To go home and perhaps start somebody back-trailing to see what happened to the rider . . . That had to be the reason. The killer did not want that tough outfit Reardon had referred to riding into town. So he had killed the horse, cut away the brand so it and its owner could not be identified, then caved dirt over it in hopes it might never be found.

If the dead man had been treated like others who had fallen in drunken fights, as the killer planned, no clue would have been left.

Picking up his hat, he went to the door. "I'll be back for supper, Bess. If you need me I'll be up on the street."

"Or at that Haley woman's place."

"Part of the job, Bess. When a man sets out to enforce the law he doesn't expect to move in the best company. Anyway, from all I hear she's not a bad woman . . . maybe not a good women, but not a bad one."

He went out quickly before Bess could reply to that, and walked slowly up the street. He stopped on the corner, thinking. People went by and nodded or spoke, and he knew how he looked to them. He wore the badge. He was authority. He was the personification of the law. He looked strong, invulnerable, capable. Yet if they only knew!

He grinned ruefully at nothing at all.

What did he have? Puggsey and Frank were definitely suspects . . . They'd undoubtedly had a fight with the victim, and might have murdered him later.

Johnny McCoy was a drunk, not always responsible for his actions, and Johnny had stabled the man's horse, knew he had gold on his person.

Time Reardon . . . a lawless, ruthless man, who also knew the stranger carried gold. A man who often went for rides in the late afternoon or evening . . . Rides to where? And for what?

He thought of old Mrs. Riggin. George had a murder in his day, too, and maybe she would know how he handled it. Any help he could get, he could use. So he would go see her . . . and he would see Mary Ann.

Oddly enough, he felt uncomfortable about that. Essentially a shy, lonely person, he had known few women. There had been a girl in Leavenworth when he was a boy, and another in Sedalia when he'd gone back there with some cattle, and then he had met Bess and after that no other girl really entered his thoughts. He had talked to Mary Ann more than once on the street, and at least once in her kitchen, but he avoided the girls, and as he wore the badge, they avoided him.

He frowned in sudden memory. People had mentioned the murder victim crossing and re-crossing the street . . . going where? The restaurant, Reardon's . . . George Blazer had seen him on the street . . . What about the bank?

What about Hyatt Johnson?

Chapter V

Leaning on an awning post in front of the General Store, Borden Chantry chewed on a match and tried to put it all together. Unwillingly, he kept thinking of Hyatt Johnson, feeling guilty all the while because he had never really liked Hyatt.

In that part of the country in that period, there was no great affection for bankers or railroad men. The former had foreclosed on too many properties when poor men were unable, due to weather and grazing conditions, to pay their bills. The latter because the rates the railroad charged were felt to be too high.

Borden Chantry, with a large ranch and a good reputation, had no success in getting a reasonable loan and reasonable rates that might have kept him in business. Hyatt had offered to buy his land at a price far below its value, or had offered a mortgage at rates he had no chance of ever paying, so Borden had refused both offers.

He had his land, but he had no cattle. He would have thought Johnson merely shortsighted if he had not known that the banker wanted his land.

Yet, the banker had to be considered. The murdered man had gone to the bank. He had been carrying money. Sometime during those few hours that money had disappeared. Had it been deposited?

If so, would Hyatt tell him? It was a common saying around town that money went into Hyatt's bank, but none came out. That wasn't, of course, literally true, yet it betrayed the town's feeling about Hyatt Johnson —for which there had been some reason.

Since he had been turned down for his loan almost a year before, Borden Chantry had not entered the bank, and his exchange of greetings on the street had always been coolly formal.

Crossing the street, he strolled up toward the bank. Ed Pearson was in town, Chantry observed, buying supplies for his mining claims. Ed lived off to the north and Chantry had intended to stop all night there when bringing Kim Baca back to jail, only Pearson had not been home.

Of a sudden, Chantry stopped and looked back, mentally estimating the load Pearson was putting on his wagon. He whistled softly . . . Ed must be doing well, for he was buying heavy, very heavy.

The interior of the bank was cool and shadowed. Lem Parkin was behind the wicket, wearing a green eyeshade and sleeve garters. "Howdy, Marshal! Don't often see you in here!"

"Not much occasion for it, Lem. My salary doesn't leave much. Is Mr. Johnson in?"

"In the office. Door's open. Just walk on back."

Hyatt Johnson was a cool, hard-eyed man with a level gaze and less expression than a hard-boiled egg. He looked up at the tall, broad-shouldered young man with no pleasure. He did want Chantry's land, and intended to have it. The ten sections Chantry owned were worth little at land prices of the day, and Hyatt Johnson knew that at the moment less valuable land was going for a dollar an acre, and sometimes less, with times the way they were. Borden Chantry's land was a different story, for he had a good creek running through it as well as several year-around water holes, and Hyatt knew a dozen men who would pay ten to twelve dollars an acre for the place, and jump at the chance. He also knew there were banks in several western towns not too far off who would give Chantry a loan with no argument, and at the best rates.

Fortunately, Chantry did not know this and Hyatt had no intention of telling him. He wanted the Chantry land. Once he had it, and he was sure he would get it eventually, he would sell off a small piece to recover whatever it cost him and hold the rest.

Borden Chantry lived off his salary, and no western marshal could be expected to live long, so Hyatt was waiting . . . not too long, he hoped.

His lips were a little dry when he looked up. Chantry wasted no time. "Hyatt," he said shortly, "I am investigating a murder."

"Murder?" Hyatt was startled. "You mean a killing?"

"I mean a murder. Tall, nice-looking man, thirty or so. Might be less. Wore a beaded buckskin jacket . . . Plains Indian-style, but I figure he came from the southwest."

Hyatt Johnson sat back in his swivel chair. "You mean you are of the opinion this was not simply a drunken brawl? A casual shooting?"

"I do. It was murder. Then the killer tried to cover it up. He changed the dead man's shirt, put on his coat. Before he put the coat on, he shot him in the chest so he would have a wound to prove he'd been shot from in front. Then he took him out and dropped him in the street."

"What has all that to do with me?"

"The first step in figuring out who killed him is to identify him, find out where he stayed, and why he came to town in the first place. Also, he was known to be carrying a poke filled with gold coins."

Hyatt Johnson shrugged. "I still can't see where I come in?"

"He was in your bank before he was killed. All I want to know is what he wanted here, and if he gave you a name."

Hyatt Johnson was disturbed. In all his dealings with ranchers he had found most of them were relatively poor business men, knowing little aside from cattle and grazing, and often with only a rudimentary knowledge of those subjects. To turn a herd of cattle loose on free range and then to make a gather and sell off the fat, mature stock required very little intelligence, as he saw it.

Now Borden Chantry was showing a brand of reasoning he had not suspected . . . pure chance, no doubt. Yet why would he take off a man's coat and shirt when he had obviously been shot?

"Yes," he replied, "I believe . . . Yes, the man was in here, but he didn't give me a name. His business, however, was confidential. I am afraid I cannot divulge any part of it."

"I'm speaking for the law, Hyatt. Not for myself."

"Nevertheless—"

Chantry stood up. "Looks like I'll have to get a court order," he said. "If that's the way you want it."

Hyatt Johnson was irritated. Now where did this cowboy ever hear of a court order? "Very well," he replied tersely, "now if that is all—?"

"For the time, Hyatt, for the time."

Borden walked back to the street, feeling his defeat. To tell the truth, he knew nothing about court orders. He had read or heard somewhere of somebody getting one to get at some papers. Well, he could try.

He would see Judge Alex McKinney.

For a few minutes he simply stood in the street. It was an easy street, lazy-seeming and dusty, too warm part of the time, too cold and windy at others, yet it had the advantage of being familiar.

He knew all the people on that street, knew what they were about. He recognized the rigs that stood there, knew the brands on the saddled stock along the hitching rail, and knew who rode most of the horses. Most of them were men he had worked with, men he knew and trusted. Yet somewhere among them was a murderer, which proved there was at least one man he did not know.

Who? Who killed the stranger, and why? Why would a man want to kill?

For gold . . . the most obvious reason, or for revenge, for fear, or over a woman. In a sudden fit of anger, maybe, in a dispute over a card game or horse-race or something. Yet a man in such a shooting had every chance of not even being arrested, and if you wished to kill a man you could find some reason for drawing on him.

Unless, of course, you knew the other man was better with a gun than you were. Or . . . even if he might be *almost* as good. Such a man might die but kill you in the process.

Sorting over what he knew, he realized that nobody had told him the whole truth. Kim Baca knew more

than he admitted, and so did both Johnny McCoy and
his son. It was very likely that Hyatt Johnson knew
enough to clear up the case.

Hyatt . . . a cool, hard, careful man. A good shot at
deer or antelope . . . or turkeys, for that matter, and a
man who always played with the odds in his favor.

Johnny, who drank too much, who was notoriously
short of money . . . and Kim Baca, who had the skill,
the intelligence, to outwit any of them. "Including me,"
he said aloud.

He had to see the judge about a court order and he
must talk to Mary Ann. He walked across to the Bon-
Ton, feeling guilty because he was procrastinating. He
was avoiding going out to Mary Ann's. Some of the
town gossips would see him going in there and their
tongues would wag.

Prissy was over from the post office. She usually
brewed her own tea in the back of the office, so if she
was here it was because she was either picking up gossip or spreading some. Still, Prissy was a good woman,
a good postmistress, and a public-spirited citizen. She
was also a good person to have on your side if it came
to politics or business about the town or country. She
not only would say what she believed, but she believed a lot of things and said it about all of them.

He sat down near the window where he could watch
the street. He knew she would be inquiring, but he was
also curious about what she had come over for. It took
no more than a minute to find out.

"Mary Ann's a sick woman, that's what Doc Terwilliger says. He says she's got consumption. She needs
rest."

Elsie Carter was over from the hotel, and she
half-turned in her chair. "Wonder some of those folks
out west wouldn't show up. Just don't know, prob'ly,
but Mary Ann Haley helped them when they needed it.
Least that's what they say."

"What's that?" Prissy demanded.

"Why, it was out Nevada way. Or maybe it was in
Montana. Smallpox hit that mining camp an' everybody come down with it. Most of the womenfolks in

town got scared and they ran. They got out, and those men that could travel, they went, too.

"There was maybe twenty, twenty-five men left in town, and most of them down with smallpox, and Mary Ann, she just pitched in an' nursed them all. She got them together in the town hall and she stayed right with them, morning, noon, an' night. Least that's what they say."

Nobody said anything for awhile, and then it was Prissy who suggested, "We could take up a collection."

Elsie shook her head. "Nobody's got much, Prissy, and there's a good many would say it was the Lord's will, what's happening to her. I doubt we could get enough for a ticket on the stage, let alone anything for her keep when she got there . . . wherever she goes."

He said nothing, staring out the window. They were right, of course, something should be done, but he also knew there was no way a collection could be gathered for Mary Ann . . . unless, he chuckled at the thought, they would do it just to get her out of town.

His thoughts returned to Johnny McCoy. With luck the Irishman might be sober now, and if he was, he might have a deal to say. He filled his cup and stared up the street, and Prissy had spoken twice to him before he realized.

"Marshal? You found who killed that man?"

"It takes awhile, ma'am. I'm workin' on it."

She sniffed. "Doesn't 'pear to me like you're doin' much but settin'."

"Now, Prissy, a man's a fool to go off half-cocked. A thing like this, a man's got to think on it. He's got to figure."

Prissy looked at him, and shook her head. "I don't know, Marshal, maybe you're not the man for the job. Why, that nice Lang Adams. We could have had him for marshal, and he's a bright man whose thoughts aren't all taken up with cows and horses."

"Lang would have been a good marshal," he admitted. "And I hear he's a good hand with a pistol. I know he can shoot turkeys."

"That's all you men think about . . . shooting. Shooting's got nothing to do with it. You've got to *think*, Marshal. Think!"

"Yes'm, I know that."

"Now, old George Riggin, he was marshal here for a long time, and a good man, too. He always said that Dover shooting was a murder, but nobody really believed him. Of course, nobody knew what George was *really* thinking. He just went about his business and if he talked to anybody it was to Helen. If he hadn't died . . . well, I always did say that if he hadn't died he would have found out who killed Pin Dover.

"Why, I talked to him just a day or two before he was killed and he told me then that he thought he had the answer . . . George wasn't one to talk. Not him. He was a stern man, and very quiet, but I'd known George more than ten years and when he was in the post office asking about some mail, he told me that he'd have the killer."

"Nonsense!" Elsie said sharply. "There was no killer. George was just a-funnin'. He did that now and again. And those folks who thought somebody did him in! Why, he just got killed by a rock slide, happens all the time!"

"Does it?" Prissy said tartly. "One day he says he'll have the killer, next day he's dead. I'd say that slide happened mighty nigh right for the killer, whoever he was."

Borden remembered the funeral. He had known old George as he had known everybody in town . . . to speak to. They had talked a time or two, and a couple of times he'd ridden on posses with the old man . . . he was no fool, George Riggin wasn't.

"Nonsense! Some folks see murder under ever' rock. Why, take that young man who got killed! I don't believe for a minute he was murdered any more than any of those drunks who get all whiskeyed up and shoot or knife each other!"

Most of them thought he was a fool, making a mystery out of something so simple. Borden Chantry looked down at his empty cup and could not remember taking those last swallows. He pushed back his chair and got up. It was time to go see Mary Ann.

"Priss," he suggested, "if you see the judge, tell him I want to see him. I'll be back in a short time."

"Ain't been down for his mail, so I reckon you'll see him right here. He coffees up whenever he gets mail and reads it whilst he drinks. But I'll tell him. Just you be back to see him when he gets here."

They all heard the shot.

It was some distance off, but it had a clear, distinct report that cut across their conversation, stilling their tongues, leaving them staring.

Shots were not uncommon at night, occasionally in the daytime, but rarely in the late afternoon before the drinkers got well started and after the hunters had come in . . . if any.

Yet there was something about that shot that hit them all, and for a moment they just stared, frightened and wondering.

Borden Chantry got up and went outside. He knew it as well as if he'd seen it happen.

Somebody else was dead.

Chapter VI

He lay sprawled at the door of the stable, his face in the fresh straw, one hand outflung and holding a bridle, the other by his side, empty.

The hands were seamed and gnarled with work, such work as even the months of hard drinking had failed to eradicate. From earliest childhood Johnny McCoy had only known work, and had never shirked his share, only to have the drink catch up to him at last.

Billy stood beside the body when they came running, his face white, his eyes wide and staring.

"Bill," Chantry put a hand on the thin shoulder, "I'm sorry, boy."

Even as he spoke he was noting the bullet hole in the side of the skull, his eyes sweeping the area for the place of the marksman.

There was no use running and chasing, for the man would be long gone, and to rush in now with a lot of would-be pursuers would only trample any evidence that might have been left.

There were a dozen men there, and as many women. Borden turned slowly to face them. "Now listen," he said loudly, "and hear me plain. You're each to go directly to your homes, and stop for nothing on the way. Go directly there and stay in until morning, or settle with me."

"What about my business?" Reardon demanded.

"One night won't hurt you," Chantry said coolly, "and I don't want everything tramped up and spoiled. With luck I'll have found what I want by daylight."

"And what'll that be?" Blazer demanded irritably.

"That's my business," Chantry replied brusquely. "Just get on home now."

"And what if we don't?" Puggsey Kern demanded.

Borden Chantry smiled. "Why, I'll throw you in jail for disturbing the peace, for loitering, and as many

50

other charges as I can find to answer the bill. But any loyal citizen who wants this mystery cleared up will do all he can to help."

"That goes with me," Lang Adams said. "Anything you need, Bord, you just call out."

Big Injun was there with the wagon, and they loaded Johnny McCoy into the back. Borden dropped his hand to Billy's shoulder. "Son, you'd better go along to my house. Bess and Tom will be mighty glad to have you with us."

Reluctantly, the boy went, stunned and silent. As yet, there had been no tears. That would come, Borden knew, when Billy was alone and away from watching eyes.

Slowly, the crowd scattered to their homes, and there they would stay . . . unless the killer was among them. For what better thing for him to do than run up and join the crowd? One by one he sorted them out in his mind, then shook his head. No . . . not in that bunch.

Hardly likely. Yet he remained uneasy. He simply did not know, and all his clues seemed to lead to nothing.

Johnny had himself been a suspect, although not a serious one in Chantry's thinking. Yet . . . he had to be considered. He had stabled the dead man's horse. He had known the man had money.

Now Johnny was dead, and the question was : . . why was he killed? What had Johnny known that the killer dared not let him tell? And Johnny was sobering up, Johnny who had always been a hard-working, loyal man.

The question now was, did Billy know what Johnny had known? Or what the killer thought he knew? If the murderer believed the boy might know something dangerous to him, the boy himself might be the next victim.

Standing in the very spot where Johnny McCoy had stood, Chantry turned slowly around, studying the angle at which the bullet must have come. Years of using guns, trying to make every shot count, and using a gun always with purpose and never for casual amuse-

ment, had taught him a good deal about guns. It had
also taught him a great deal about the men who use
guns.

This man was shooting to kill, not to frighten or
wound. Therefore he must have been confident of his
marksmanship, as well as of his position. It was still
light, so the man must have been concealed, must have
fired, then abandoned his position instantly. He must
have abandoned it in such a way that he would not be
noticed, or if noticed his presence would surprise no one.

Rarely is anyone unobserved, even when they are
most sure they are unseen. There is nearly always an
eye to see, and often a mind to wonder.

Hence the unknown marksman had to select a concealed position to which he could gain access without
being seen, or if seen it had to be a position where
his presence would not require explanation.

Johnny, of course, might have turned as the bullet
struck. Might even have been starting to bend down.
The bullet holes had seemed to be slightly slanted down
as though fired from a slightly higher elevation.

Borden Chantry stood with his hands on his hips,
looking around. If the killer had remained in firing
position he would now have him, Chantry, under the
gun. And he had already been shot at once.

Slowly he turned. There were two second-story windows in the bank building from which a bullet could
have come. There was one over the stage station office,
allowing for some movement from Johnny after he was
shot, and there were two or three barns. These barns
each had a loft with doors or windows from which
shots might have been fired. All were within two hundred yards—no great distance, certainly.

He prowled about, going from barn to barn, studying
distances and elevations. At last he halted and stared
around with disgust. What was he trying to do? He
was no investigator. Of course, it was like tracking, and
he had done a lot of that. Walking back to the McCoy
cabin he sat down on the stoop.

It had become dark. Only a few stars were out, and it
was clouding up.

Suppose . . . just suppose the killer *had* done as he

at first thought? Suppose the killer had fired his shot, then run down to the body?

If he had done that, then what had become of his rifle?

Borden Chantry got up quickly. His asking people to go home had been in hopes no tracks would be made to cover up those he was looking for. But suppose that had trapped the killer? For if the killer had run down to the body, then he had left his rifle either at or near the spot from which the shot had been fired!

Moreover, he must return and get that rifle before he, Borden Chantry, could find it.

If that was true then before many hours were past the killer must leave his living quarters, wherever they might be and slip through the streets and alleys, get the rifle and get back to his room!

Borden Chantry walked into the street and stood there for a moment, making a mental picture of the town. Yet the more he sized up the situation the less he liked it. There had been no real clue in the position of the body of the original victim, but with McCoy it was different, and it offered possibilities. Too many possibilities.

From where McCoy had fallen he could have been shot from any one of six directions and Chantry could eliminate none of them offhand. The trouble was that a man shot dead does not always drop in his tracks. He might have made a full turn, a half turn, or just turned his head, so the angle of the wound was of slight help, no more.

Sighting from the spot where the body had fallen, there was a direct line of sight to the bank . . . the rear door of the bank or either of two upstairs windows. There was also a direct line from the back door or window of the Corral Saloon.

Lines could also be laid out to Mary Ann Haley's, the back of the stage company office, the stage company corrals and stable, as well as the back of the restaurant. There were just too many possibilities.

When it came to that, there was a direct line of sight from his own kitchen to the spot where McCoy fell.

Irritably, he shook away the thought. Bess? It was impossible. Yet out of fairness he must suspect everybody.

If only he could come upon some clue to the man's identity.

Borden Chantry walked slowly up the dusty street, and turning aside, walked toward the rear corner of the Corral Saloon. The shot could have been fired from here. Carefully, he checked the area . . . No fresh tracks that he could make out, no cartridge shell, no indication that anyone had stood there.

He crossed the street to the café and went between it and the post office, then walked along behind the buildings to the rear of the stage office. He had no reason to think Blazer might have shot McCoy, but he could not rule it out, either, so he scouted the area thoroughly, then around the corral and the barn where spare horses were kept for the stages.

Nothing.

The night was cool. It was clouding over, and it would be a dark night. Glancing toward the lights of his own windows he thought he saw his wife's shadow against the curtain. She would be feeding the youngsters about now, his own son Tom, and Billy McCoy.

Two men murdered . . . and they might be separate and distinctive crimes, but he did not believe it. He walked back between the store and the jail and out on the boardwalk.

The street was empty as the street of a ghost town. The people were cooperating, and that was a help. No cowboys in town during the week, to speak of.

He crossed the street to the rear corner of the bank, and drew another blank. There was no chance of getting upstairs until tomorrow. He glanced past the corner toward Hyatt Johnson's house, a fine, big, well-built house such as befitted a banker. And a house from which the bullet might have been fired.

He was turning away when he saw, beyond a couple of residences, the vast dark bulk of the old Simmons Freight Barn. The Simmons outfit had operated bull trains out of that barn, freighting to the western mining camps, and east and north to the railroad. A year before they had closed up shop and gone out of business, selling out when the railroad built on west. Now the place was empty.

Or was it?

It was by far the largest building in town, yet he had not even thought of it, for it stood empty and was somehow no longer even a topic of conversation. Yet from that building, from either the front of the building or from the loft, it would have been an easy shot—not over seventy yards, at best, from where McCoy fell.

He started to cross to the old barn, then turned abruptly away and went across the street to the café. A light still showed there, and he could see Ed washing up.

He opened the door and stepped in.

"Marshal? Just closing up. You sure killed business tonight!"

"Sorry."

"Don't be. I can stand the rest. I got me a good book and some drummer passin' through left me a bunch of newspapers from Omaha and St. Louis. I surely do like readin' them papers. It fair worries a body to see what the world is comin' to! Why, the crime in them cities! You couldn't give 'em to me. I'd rather live here where it's safe."

"Wasn't very safe for Johnny McCoy."

Ed's face was serious. "It surely wasn't. Marshal, I liked that man. Like I said, he was a warm, generous fella, give you the shirt off his back. If you catch the man who did it, I'd like a hand on the rope."

"I'll get him." Chantry spoke with confidence, and surprised himself, for it was a confidence he did not feel. Or did he? Where had that quick reply come from? He was never a man given to making flat statements of what or what not he would do. Yet the words had come as if springing from a deep well of belief within himself.

"I've got to get him, Ed. This is a good town, a law-abiding town, and I took an oath to keep it so. We've had shootings and cuttings, but mostly not among the townfolk, and there's a change of feeling, Ed. The old days are gone."

"Marshal, I'm going to leave the door open. There's some meat on that tray, along with some bread and butter. There's coffee in the pot . . . fresh-made. I had me an idea you'd be around most of the night, so I made it for you.

"Yonder in the case there's a half of apple pie. Be stale tomorrow. You he'p yourself. I'm going to turn in now."

"All right. Mind if I keep one light burning?"

"Figured on it. Night, Marshal. See you tomorrow."

Borden Chantry carried the pot from the stove to a table along with some slices of meat, bread, and a quarter of the pie.

The light was in the kitchen, and where he sat it was in the shadow. It was dim and quiet, the room smelling faintly of coffee. Straddling a chair, he reached around the back and put a thick sandwich together. Then with his right hand he reached back and took the thong off his gun.

Facing the street from the darkened room, he ate his sandwich and sipped coffee, ears tuned for any slightest sound, eyes for any movement.

The old building creaked slightly as the heat left it. A lone dog trotted across the street, pausing to sniff some object lying in the gutter. Gradually, his eyes became more and more accustomed to the dark, and from where he sat, invisible himself, he could look northeast past the corner of the bank toward Hyatt's house, across the street at the Corral Saloon, lighted but empty, and southwest past the rear of the Mexican restaurant toward Mary Ann's.

The kitchen was on his left, the wall of the building behind him, and beyond that the dark area that divided the restaurant building from where his own home stood.

He ate his sandwich, drank his coffee, and then poured a new cup and tied into the apple pie. He was lifting the second bite to his mouth when his eye caught a faint shifting of shadows near the rear of the bank.

For a moment he was very still. Had he deceived himself? Had something really moved? Or—?

He put down his fork and wiped his hands on the rough napkin. He got up, stepping back from the chair, and on cat feet he went to the door.

Nothing moved.

Yet he had seen something. Was it the old dog? His mind told him no.

The door opened easily under his hand, with only the faintest of squeaks. He stepped out on the boardwalk, crossed it with one more step and started across the street vaguely lit by the light from the Corral Saloon. He swore softly. If anybody was watching, they could not help but see him.

The saloon seemed empty. There was no sign of anybody around. He went quickly to the corner and looked past it toward Mary Ann's . . . A shadow moved against the curtain, but there was no sound of music. Then he remembered. Mary Ann was ill.

The Mexican café was dark.

Holding close to the wall of the saloon, he walked toward the rear, and looking past the corner he could see the great bulk of the Simmons barn. All was black and silent.

He rested a hand on his gun, straining his eyes toward the old barn. Yet he saw nothing . . . it was something he *heard*.

Something he *felt*.

Hesitating only a second, heart pounding, he crossed toward the barn. His toe kicked a small pebble and it rattled against others. He swore mentally, reached the corner of the barn and edged along toward the door.

It stood open . . . only a few inches.

He drew a long breath, felt his mouth go dry and his heart pounding in slow, measured beats, and then he stepped through into the darkness.

He felt the blow coming before it hit him. He started to turn, and then something smashed down on his skull and he felt himself falling . . . falling . . . falling. . . .

Chapter VII

He grabbed out wildly, seizing upon a boot, but the foot kicked free and he heard running steps. He yelled out, started to rise, then fell back into the straw.

He must have passed out then because the next he knew, several people were standing over him and Prissy was holding his head.

Time Reardon was there, Lang Adams and Alvarez from the Mexican café.

"I hear you yell, señor," Alvarez said. "I grab a gun. I come to help, but there is nobody, only you on the ground."

He got up shakily, his skull buzzing. "Thanks, I'll be all right."

Prissy stood back, and as he raised his eyes, Borden could see somebody . . . Hyatt, undoubtedly . . . standing in the door of his house, light streaming past him, looking to see what the confusion was about.

"I got slugged," he explained. "Somebody was in the barn."

"Did you see him?" Reardon demanded. "Did you get a look at him?"

"No . . . no, I didn't. I was lucky not to get killed."

"You've got a thick skull," Lang said, grimly. "Or you would be dead. Bord, if you're going to keep on with this, you should have a deputy. You could get yourself killed."

"I . . . I'll make out." He shook his head but it buzzed. "I'm all right. I'll just go along home."

"You'd better wake up Doc Terwilliger," Lang advised. "You've got a nasty cut on your skull."

"Bess will take care of it. She's had experience." Somebody handed him his hat and he checked his gun. Still in its holster. "You all go along home now. I'll be all right."

Lang hesitated. "Bord? If I can help . . . ?"

"Thanks, Lang. I'll be all right."

When they had gone he turned to the Mexican, who was the last to leave. "Alvarez?"

He turned. "Sí?"

"Were you the first one here?"

"Sí . . . I think so, señor."

"Did you see anything? Anybody?"

"I . . . think . . . maybe. Somebody was in the barn, I think. I hear somebody, and there was a light . . . then a curse. Curses . . . then somebody ran.

"Señor?" Alvarez looked up at him. "I think there were *two* people in there. I hear curses, then like a scramble and I am coming running, and something moved . . . very quick . . . and was gone."

"You didn't get a look at him . . . or her?"

"No, señor."

"Thanks, Alvarez. You got out there mighty fast."

"Sí . . . you are the law, señor, and the law is good to have. There are savages among us, señor. Without the law there is no freedom, there is no safety. I am for the law, señor."

When he had gone Borden Chantry walked into the barn, whose door now stood wide ajar. All was very still. He felt along the wall to where he knew a lantern had hung . . . It was still there.

He raised the globe and, striking a match, lit the lantern. For a moment he just looked around. The old stable had that musty smell of a place kept closed, mingled with the smell of hay and the leftover smell of harness now gone.

He walked slowly around, glancing into the stalls, at the ladder to the loft, and the dirt floor at its foot. He stopped by the ladder . . . nothing. He looked up into the black square of the trapdoor and decided against it.

At the back there was a tack room and a smaller door, and beside that door a barrel with several sticks in it and a wornout broom. A sack lay on the floor near it.

A rifle could have been placed there and hidden under the sack. Yet there were a number of places in which it might have been concealed. No doubt, it was gone now.

After awhile, his head throbbing painfully, Chantry walked home, pausing to lean against a building at one point, his head feeling heavy and awkward.

Bess met him at the door, her face shocked at his expression.

"Oh, Borden! Borden, what happened? You've been shot!"

"Not shot." He tried to grin. "Just rapped on the skull. I'd better sit down, Bess."

She helped him to a chair, then went to the sink for water. It felt good just to sit down. He leaned his head back and closed his eyes. In a moment he felt the soothing touch of the warm cloth as Bess dabbed away the matted blood in his hair.

"It's a nasty cut, Borden, and it's all discolored . . . bruised."

"I'll be all right. He was waiting for me, just inside the freight barn."

"Who was it, Borden?"

"I wish I knew . . . But I've a clue. A small clue, but a clue."

"What is it, Borden?"

"No . . . not now. I'd rather not say, and you'd think it too unimportant . . . And maybe it is." He got up unsteadily. "I'm going to bed, Bess. All I need is rest."

The gray, slivery wood of the boardwalks was hot to the touch. The dusty street was empty and still. It was just short of noon, and the town was quiet, waiting, listening.

Judge McKinney sat in the Bon-Ton over an early lunch. He was a big old man in a threadbare gray suit, the vest spotted from food spills at some bygone meal. Under his black hat his hair was gray and thick, his beard the same.

"Sorry to hear about Borden Chantry," he said to Hyatt Johnson. "He's a good man."

"A good rancher . . . At least he was. But do you

think he's the man for this job, Judge? Why, he told me yesterday he planned to get a court order from you to examine the bank files. That's unheard of!"

"Not quite, Hyatt. Not quite. It's been done a time or two, and Borden's not a man to go off on a tangent. If he wants to see your files he no doubt has good reason."

"But I can't let—"

Judge McKinney leveled his cool gray eyes at Johnson. "Hyatt, if I write a court order for Borden Chantry to see your files, he'll see them."

Hyatt Johnson hesitated. That was not what he wanted, not what he wanted at all. He had been so sure that a word to the judge . . . Well, he was the banker, and the judge was the authority. Weren't they on the same side? He hesitated, waiting just a moment, then he said, "Judge, I'd never refuse a court order, of course. But the files have confidential information . . . I am sure you wouldn't want everybody having access to your personal financial information, nor would I. I think—"

"Hyatt," McKinney smiled, "I doubt if there's anything in those files that Borden Chantry doesn't know. As for my finances, I venture to say that Priscilla could give you a clearer statement on them than you could . . . or I, for that matter.

"In a town of this size there are no secrets, and I am sure that if Borden Chantry wants information, he should have it."

"Perhaps." Hyatt Johnson was irritated, and McKinney noticed it. "I sometimes think he's getting too big a sense of self-importance. Why, he's taking a simple shooting and building it all out of proportion! You'd think the President had been shot!"

"And why not?" McKinney sipped his coffee, then wiped his moustache. "Is not every man important in his own way? Which one of us is not important to someone? I daresay to his family that murdered man was more important than any president.

"Hyatt, self-importance can come to all of us. We have to view things in perspective. I sometimes think

that what most bankers need is a few years of reading
philosophy, or to get out of the bank and punch
cows or trade horses or something.

"Borden Chantry, right at this moment and in this
town, is the most important man in our lives."

Hyatt stared. Was the judge losing his mind?

"I mean what I say, Hyatt. That young man is all
that stands between us and savagery. He's the thin line
of protection, and when he walks out there on the
street his life is on the line every minute he wears that
badge.

"We are free to come and go, to make love, do business, buy groceries, play cards, have a drink now and
again because he is there. He is our first line of defense
. . . in many respects, the only line.

"The savage is never far from the surface in any of
us, but because we know he is there we fight it down.
I don't lose my temper and strike somebody because
he is there. The drifting cowboy with a chip on his
shoulder avoids trouble, because he is there.

"We have freedom, you and I and Priscilla and
Elsie and all of us, because Borden Chantry is out
there with that badge. To tell you the truth, I think he
is the man who should wear it, beyond all others.

"He would shoot . . . I happen to know that he has
. . . but he has the cool judgment to know when it is
not necessary. He has the quiet strength that makes
people believe him. He doubts himself, and that is often
good, but he does not doubt his ability to handle a
situation. He's roped too many wild steers, ridden too
many broncs, handled too many tough men to do
that.

"I trust him, Hyatt, and you had better do the same.
Some people believe the law to be a restriction . . . It
is a restriction only against evil. Laws are made to free
people, not to bind them—if they are the proper laws.
They tell each of us what he may do without trans-
gressing on the equal liberty of any other man."

"I never thought of it in just that way."

"I notice, Hyatt, that you do not wear a gun. Why
not?"

"Why, I never thought it necessary. After all, I am a

banker . . . a businessman. I have no need for a gun."

Judge McKinney smiled. "That's right . . . Ordinarily you wouldn't have any use for one, and that's because Borden Chantry does have one and he is paid to use it for you. .

"You can do business because he is protecting you. There was a time when no man was safe in this town unless armed, and that time may come again. In the meanwhile we have Borden Chantry. My advice to you, Hyatt, is cooperate."

Judge McKinney brushed the crumbs from his vest. "Hyatt, if Borden wants a court order from me, he'll get it. Why make it necessary?"

"Suppose I preferred not to accept your court order?"

McKinney smiled. "You're too smart for that, Hyatt. Because if you refused a court order of mine, I'd have Borden throw you in jail along with Kim Baca. And, like him, you'd wait for the session of court."

"You'd do that to me?"

"Why not to you? Or any man?" McKinney swallowed coffee and put his cup down. "If you want me to go to the trouble of preparing that court order, you do it, but if I were you I'd just find Borden Chantry and help him all you can. One of these days you may need him almighty bad."

After Hyatt had gone, Ed came in from the kitchen. "Couldn't help but overhear," he commented.

"Nothing secret. A few items the good banker did not quite grasp. You got a couple more of them doughnuts, Ed? They taste mighty good, and Borden's not here yet."

Borden Chantry awakened to a dull headache, and for a time he lay still, staring up at the flowered wallpaper. A little sunlight came in through the window, and the curtain stirred in the faint breeze.

After a moment he closed his eyes, vaguely listening to the sounds from the kitchen where Bess was at work. It was good to just lie still.

Yet lying still solved no crimes, and they were expecting him to be out on the street.

He sat up, very carefully, and swung his feet to the floor. His head swam a little, but waiting just a moment, he stood up. Hand on the foot of the bed, he stood still, trying to see how his body would react, yet as he stood there he saw some straw on the windowsill.

Straw, crushed together by a small bit of mud or manure.

On Bess's windowsill? It was absurd. She was the most careful woman he had ever known about her house . . . Yet it was there. And the fact of its presence could only mean that somebody had come through that window since Bess had cleaned the room, even since she had last seen it.

She had gotten up in the dark this morning, not to disturb him, and would not have seen it in the dark last night. That meant that yesterday somebody had come through that window, somebody who had been in a corral or barn.

Yet in the daytime such a person would have been seen. And anyway, the house was open.

Which implied the entry had been made last night, and before he was put to bed in here.

There had been somebody in the barn last night, there had been two people, at least. *Had one of them come from his own home?*

That was impossible!

Yet, the straw was there. True, there were twenty places, even fifty places from which it might have come.

Why through the window? For how else could it have gotten on the sill? Surely Bess . . . Bess would have come right in the door, no need for anything else. He had not been home, and Tom would undoubtedly have been asleep.

Billy McCoy?

Suppose Billy had been out? This window in this room would have been a good place to re-enter the house, for this room would be empty, that side of the house obscured. As the parlor, or front room as it was called, was only used when the preacher came calling or some such occasion, Billy would not have dreamed of using that door, and the kitchen door squeaked.

Billy, no doubt . . . But why? Why in the middle of the night and to the stable?

Slowly, carefully, so as not to jolt his head and start it aching more violently, Borden Chantry dressed, pulled on his boots and slung his gun belt around him. He checked the load of his gun as he always did, even when it had not been used in some time.

He walked into the kitchen, and through the window he could see Billy out there with Tom, throwing a loop at a post. Tame stuff for Billy, who had done some roping, but good practice for Tom, who was younger.

Bess turned quickly. "Borden! You shouldn't be up! Doctor Terwilliger said—"

"I can imagine what he said. How's about a cup of coffee?"

"Sit down . . . *please!*" She glanced at him, then poured the coffee. "You've no idea how pale you are. You mustn't go out there, Borden, it's turned hot."

"Just a few odds and ends," he said. "I'll be all right." She put the pot back on the stove. "Hear anything around last night, Bess?"

"Around here?" She turned her back to the stove. "No. Was there something?"

"Don't mention it, but I thought Billy might have gone out."

"Billy? Of course not! Well . . . I didn't see him go out."

They discussed it quietly, keeping their voices low. Did Billy know something he did not? He should ask him, but now was not the time. Sometime when he wasn't playing with Tom and when they could be alone, man-to-man style.

"Oh!" Bess suddenly remembered. "Kim Baca wants to see you, and Hyatt Johnson asked for you to drop in when you could. He said to tell you he'd had a talk with the judge."

Kim Baca . . . ?

Chapter VIII

Borden Chantry walked slowly out to the street, then turned left and was passing the restaurant when Lang rapped on the window. He went in.

Prissy was there, over a cup of tea with Elsie, and Borden sat down opposite Lang.

"You should be in bed," Lang said. "I'm waiting for Blossom."

"She coming in?"

"She's in. She's got a sick hand out to the place and wanted to talk to Doc about him." Lang looked at him. "Man, you must've taken a rap. Who would ever think anybody'd be in an old barn?"

"I knew there was somebody there," Chantry said, absently, "but I wasn't expecting to get rapped on the skull."

"You *knew*?"

"Sure. Trouble was there were two somebodys there, and I don't think one of them knew the other was there."

"I'd stay out of dark corners if I were you, Bord. Somebody is out to get you, that's plain enough."

He paused. "If you need help, Bord, I'd be glad to serve. So would some of the others. That way you could get some rest and the town would be protected, too."

"I've got help."

"You have? Who?"

"The killer himself. He's scared. Something I've done, or something he thinks I am about to do has him running scared. He killed McCoy before he could talk to me. Johnny was sobering up. Now you know Johnny. He's been hitting the bottle hard, so if he was sobering up there had to be a reason. He knew something, and he was going to tell me, but if I know Johnny, he

66

wouldn't trust himself to remember or not to get drunk again, so he'd have written it down."

"Or told Billy."

"No, he wouldn't tell Billy. Kids talk too much, and then he wouldn't want the boy in jeopardy. He would have left a record, somehow.

"You know Johnny and I worked together, and Johnny worked for me a time or two, also. A couple of times when he could feel the urge coming on, he got in touch with me or with somebody, or left written word so we'd be able to take care of the cattle.

"He might have had a weakness, but along with it he had a sense of responsibility . . . And Johnny knew how I feel about the law."

"You'd better get to his house before the killer does, then."

"I'll get there. Don't worry about that." Chantry pushed back from the table. "I've got to get up the street. I've got to see Hyatt."

Prissy stopped him at the door, and said, very softly, "Borden, old Mrs. Riggin was asking me to have you stop by. She's mighty poorly these days, and you know she and George always had a warm feeling for you."

He felt a sharp sense of guilt. "I know . . . and I haven't been by to see her. I'll do that . . . today."

"Now, Borden. Do it now. She's quite worried about you, and she was insistent that you come by."

"Well," he hesitated, irritated by the necessity. He had to see Hyatt. If the banker had sent for him it almost certainly meant that he was willing to tell what he knew. Moreover, he did not feel like walking and was not up to saddling a horse. "All right, I'll go."

As he walked outside, Time Reardon was standing on the walk in front of his Corral Saloon. He took the cigar from his mouth and watched Chantry up the street, and Borden was aware of his gaze. There was no sign of Kern or Hurley, but without doubt they were close by.

Big Injun was sitting in front of the jail, and that reminded Borden of Kim Baca, who also wished to see him. Yet there was only so much a man could do. Reluctantly, he crossed the street to the bank side, then walked across the lot south of it and past the Jenkins house, which was the next one to Hyatt's own home, which was almost half a block further along, and by itself.

Mrs. Riggin's house was a small, pleasant and flower-girdled house on the edge of a small patch of woods. He opened the gate and went up the walk. When he rapped on the door he heard her steps, quite slow and feeble now, as she came to the door.

He removed his hat, and stood waiting, hoping his hair wasn't mussed. She opened the door and smiled weakly. "Borden Chantry, you naughty boy! You haven't been by to see me!"

"I reckon not, ma'am. I been busy, but I was figurin' on—"

"Bosh! You'd forgotten all about me! Well, come in an' set. I've got some of those ginger cookies you used to set store by. Can't make 'em like I used to, but when I had to see you I just put together a batch of 'em, just like I used to when you was a boy."

She put a blue and white dish with a dozen cookies on the table, and sat down in her old rocker with the antimacassar on the back. Borden lowered himself gingerly into a chair opposite her.

George Riggin had been a tall, thin old man, forty or fifty pounds lighter than Chantry, and Borden never trusted the chairs. They always seemed too flimsy.

"Borden, you're a busy man so I'm not about to waste your time with chitchat. Folks tell me you're huntin' the man who killed that stranger, and who now has prob'ly killed Johnny McCoy.

"Johnny was a good boy, a real good boy. Used to run errands for me, like you done. He rode with George a time or two, too. George trusted him . . . used to talk to him some. More'n he ever talked to me, even.

"George never felt like crime was a woman's affair, but he talked of some of his cases with Johnny. Johnny knows a good bit of what George was thinkin', too.

"Like that Pin Dover killin'. George was sure it was

murder. He done tol' me that much. Murder, he says, out-an'-out murder! And I heard him say as much to Johnny.

"Why should anybody kill Pin? He was harmless enough. Given to driftin', never much account 'cept as a cowpuncher. Tried mindin' other jobs here and yon but he never done much good at 'em. Yet there he was . . . murdered.

"George said it was done a-purpose by somebody Pin didn't even know. So why should he be killed? George asked himself that question and the only answer he could get was that Pin had been killed for something he knew, or something somebody thought he knew.

"George was a pretty good detective, you know. He had the patience for it. He always said there was no such thing as a perfect crime, just imperfect investigations, and he was determined to stay with the Pin Dover case until he had found the guilty man. He was gettin' close, too. That's why he was killed."

"You think he was murdered?"

"I know it. I tried to tell them but they thought I was just a silly old woman. And then, when they finally went out to look around, the ground was all trampled up . . . right up to the edge of that bank."

She put her cup down. "Borden, you've been working with cattle since you were big enough to straddle a horse. Did you ever see a herd of twenty or thirty head go right up to the edge of a bank unless they were driven?

"It was cattle wiped all those footprints out, and whatever sign there may have been, cattle hooves, obviously driven by somebody, because you know cows would walk along the rim if they had to. But a herd of them would never go right up there unless somebody was pushing them . . . No reason for them to go. The grass was all et off up there, and the cow trail led around the foot of the cliff where George rode."

Borden put down his cup. George Riggin was no fool. A mighty cool head, and so was his wife. He'd known Ma Riggin since he was knee-high and she'd never been addled . . . a bright, interested, lively old lady. When you came to think of it, getting hit by a falling rock in this country was about the last way you'd expect a man to die.

"Did he ever give you any idea who he suspected? Or had he gone that far?"

"I think he had a mighty good idea. No, he never talked about his cases at home, on'y once in a while he'd say something. If anybody knew what he thought, it was Johnny McCoy. That was why Johnny came to me the other day."

"Came to *you?* Johnny did?"

"Yes, sir! He surely did. He come in here in a hurry. He said he was wishful of talking to you, confidential, and could I get you up here so's he could meet you accidental-like. He said he had reasons for not wanting to walk right up to you."

"Was he sober?"

"Well, he was comin' off a drunk, if you know what I mean. You know, Johnny started to sober up right there before he was killed. He was right worried about something but he wouldn't tell me what it was. He said George never wanted to get me involved and he had no right to. But he had to see you . . . right off. I mean, he was in a hurry, Borden. And then he was dead. Right after he left here."

Borden shifted uneasily in his chair, and it creaked under him. Warily, he took up his cup. Dover, Riggin, the stranger, and now McCoy . . . Four unexplained killings in less than a year, and two of them right close together.

"I wish George was here," he said. "I'm no detective. I'm not really much good as a lawman, Ma. I just keep order and throw a drunk in jail now and again, so's he can sleep it off."

"Don't fret, son. George thought you were just the man for the job. Said you were persistent, and that was what it took."

He put down his cup. There was so much he did not know. So many things were more important than just walking the streets with a badge.

Men had been murdered here. True, it was a violent

time, yet that was passing, and this town was evidence of it. The dusty streets, the few scattered buildings, already weatherbeaten while yet so new, these were a bulwark against desolation. This was a place where people met to trade, to exchange ideas, to pray, to learn. Even this shabby little trail town had its civic pride, its love of home, its desire to become better.

For death to occur was natural, and in a violent land a violent death was more to be expected than otherwise. This did not necessarily mean a death by the gun or arrow, but one might die in a multitude of other ways, all violent.

To fall ahead of stampeding cattle, to be gored by an angry steer or a cow, to be thrown and trampled by a wild mustang, to be frozen to death or to die of thirst, these were the order of the day. Yet there were dozens of other ways in which a man might die on the plains or in the mountains, and men accepted these ways.

It was customary to settle disputes between men with weapons. The pistol was the most prevalent weapon and the one most often used.

Murder was quite another thing. It was more than a crime against an individual, it was a crime against society, against its accepted customs, its way of thinking. To permit such a killer to go unpunished would be a blow to the world they were struggling to build.

"Ma," he said wearily, "I want to do my job. If I find the murderer he will have to stand trial. I wouldn't want to arrest a man without sufficient evidence, but I'm worried. Whoever he is, something's bothering him, and I think he will kill again, and I think he's one of us . . . somebody right here in town."

"Can't never tell. Way I heard it, that dead man had money when he come to town . . . Where is it now? You can bet that whoever has it will want to spend it. What Pa always said. 'You let a thief have money,' he used to say, 'and there ain't one in fifty can keep it hid. They got to go out an' live high on the hog . . . All you got to do is watch.'"

"I can't wait. Somebody else will die. Anyway, Time Reardon hinted that if the dead man was who he

thought it might be, we might have somebody comin'
in here huntin' him. Somebody who would set the
town on its ear."

"You let 'em come. We got Winchesters enough in
this town to fight us a war, and there's enough fightin'
men here to handle 'em.

"This here town is like most western towns. Hyatt
Johnson, now, he was a major in the Rebel cavalry.
Sure, he's a banker now, but he's got him a rifle hung
up back of his desk and he's got a thirty-six Navy in
his desk drawer.

"Blazer over at the express office was a sharpshooter
with Sherman, and he fit in three, four Indian battles.
Ain't hardly a man in any western town who wasn't in
the war on one side or t'other, and most have fit Injuns
since they were boys . . . An' most of them shot meat
for the table. Anybody comes into one of these towns
huntin' trouble, he's askin' for a stakeout on Boot
Hill."

Mrs. Riggin paused. "Borden, you should talk to
young Billy McCoy. Now there's a quick-witted youngster. Like his pa used to be, maybe more so. He sees
nearly everything goes on around town, and believe
me, Johnny knew something he was itching to tell
you. It was something that scared him."

"I'll talk to him." Chantry got up, turning his hat in
his hands. "You've got no idea who George suspected?"

"No, I don't, but George was a painstaking man,
Borden. You remember that? He was not a man to
leave things to chance, nor was he a trusting man.

"I mean, George liked people, but he expected little
from them. He often said all people were human, all
could make mistakes. And many people had a little
larceny in them, given the chance. George trusted no
man to be free from error, and most particularly, himself."

Borden got up and moved toward the door, yet
something in her words caught at his attention. He
turned slowly. "Ma? Did George ever keep any notes?
I mean, when he was working on a case? Did he
keep it all in his head?"

"Well . . . mostly. But not always, Borden. And on

this last case I think he kept notes, but I never saw them. Like I said, he never talked much about his cases around home. Only once in awhile he'd come out with something or tell me where he was going. Like the day he was killed."

"Where was he going?" Even as Chantry asked the question it came as a shock that he had no idea . . . that so far as he knew nobody had ever inquired. He himself had not yet been appointed marshal and he had heard of Riggin's death only at secondhand. He'd been busy trying to save something on his own ranch.

"Out to see Blossom. They were old friends, you know. He and Ed Galey rode the trail together, bringing cattle up from Chihuahua, and he'd been studying about seeing her for some time, then finally decided on it. He was riding to see her when he was killed."

Chantry turned the knob, opening the door to leave. Mrs. Riggin got up from her rocker. "Oh . . . I almost forgot! George said Johnny McCoy was to have that fancy bridle of his, and Billy was to have his spurs, but he said most particular that you were to have his saddle.

"Said it might need mending a bit, but you were a good hand at that sort of thing, and would fix it better'n new. If you want, you can pick it up now."

He thanked her, then walked out on the porch. For a moment he stood there, looking about. His head ached, felt like something was pressing down on his right over the eyebrows. He ran his fingers through his hair, then put on his hat.

Oh, yes . . . the saddle.

He walked around the house and into the small barn. The bridle was hanging on a nail where George always kept it. The spurs were on the table.

The saddle was gone.

Chapter IX

In the dust of the barn floor there were boot tracks.

Borden Chantry looked sharply around. No place to hide in the barn. He ran outside, glancing quickly around. Nothing moved nearer than the street, but there was brush at the back of the barn, and a path, he recalled, that ran to the bottom of the arroyo.

Turning, he ran toward the path. Something crashed in the brush. He thought he heard running footsteps, then drawing a pistol, he ran after them.

The arroyo broke into several branches, and he skated to a stop, listening. No sound . . . not a whisper. He started toward one branch, then halted. He glanced around for tracks, but at this point the floor of the arroyo was almost one sheet of solid rock. He swore softly, then walked up the nearest arroyo.

It twisted and turned away from town. Walking back, he tried a second. It led back toward the hills. The other branch wound north along the back of the town, and he should have thought of it at once. There were a dozen places where a man could emerge with small chance of being seen, and whoever had grabbed the saddle had gotten away.

But what of the saddle itself? A man does not run lightly and easily while carrying a heavy stock saddle.

Walking back to where he heard the crash in the brush, it took him only a few minutes to find it. Obviously, whoever had stolen the saddle had thrown it aside to enable him to get away. Borden shouldered the sadde and walked away from the arroyo, past the house and into the street.

He was tired, and the running had started his head to aching again. He crossed the street to the Bon-Ton and went in. He did not want anything to eat, and he did not want coffee. He wanted only to sit down, just for a moment.

Dropping into the first chair, he stared around him, suddenly dizzy. Ed crossed the room and put down a pot and a cup. "You all right, Marshal? You look done in?"

"It's that rap on the skull. I must have had a mild concussion when I got hit the other night. I'll just sit here a moment until I feel better."

"Take your time. Did you see Hyatt? He was askin' for you."

"I'll see him later."

"Looks like George Riggin's saddle," Ed commented. "He sure set store by it, but it ain't as good as yours."

"He wanted me to have it."

"Well, I guess a man can use an extry saddle oncet in awhile. He sure give that one some wear. That ol' saddle could tell some stories, given a chance and a tongue."

Ed walked back to the kitchen and Borden lowered his head to his arms. Only for a minute. If he could just rest for a minute.

"Bord?" It was Lang's voice.

He looked up. "Sit down, Lang. I'm just resting a bit."

"You look all in," Lang's voice was worried. "Bord, you've got to take it easy. In your condition you shouldn't be out running around. After all, if you're right about this and it is a local man he isn't going anywhere. You're just killing yourself for nothing."

"You're right. Bess tells me the same thing. Have some coffee?"

Lang filled their cups. Bord leaned back in his chair. He had always envied Lang, a cool, confident man who knew where he was going and what he wished to do.

"It's hot out there," Lang commented. "With that head you're carrying it could make you sick." He glanced at the saddle. "What's the idea? You going someplace?"

"It was George Riggin's saddle. He wanted me to have it."

"Why? You've got a saddle."

Borden shrugged. "A man likes to pass something on. He left his spurs to Billy McCoy."

"You know, Bord," Lang paused. "I've been thinking about Billy. When Blossom and I are married, we could take the boy out to the ranch. He'd like it there, and he could be a help to us in summer, and could go to school in winter. We'd like to make a home for him."

"Have you mentioned it to Blossom?"

"Oh, sure! She's all for it. You know Blossom, got a heart as big as the world and she always liked Johnny, anyway. In fact, she and Johnny were old friends."

"I suppose so. This is a big country but there's mighty few people. Sooner or later everybody knows everybody . . . and everything about everybody."

Lang glanced at him. "Why do you say that?"

"Well, you know how it is. There's no secrets in a country where there are so few people. An eastern man might think he could come out here and lose himself, but he'd be wrong. A man can't move in this country without somebody knowing."

Lang sipped his coffee. "Then catching your man should be easy, shouldn't it?" He smiled. "If there's anything I can do to help, just call on me. Any riding, asking questions . . . anything of the sort."

"Thanks, Lang. I appreciate that." Chantry got to his feet. "I've got to see Hyatt, but it will have to wait. Bess will be worried about me."

"Want me to come along? Or if you want to see Hyatt now, I could carry your saddle home for you. Keep it in the barn, don't you?"

"Yeah, but I'll take it. I'm only a few steps away now."

He took up the saddle on one arm and went out the door. The full weight of the sun struck him like a blow. For a moment he stood still, closing his eyes against the glare. Then he walked to the corner of the café and, turning it, walked back to his own house.

Bess opened the door for him. "Borden! I've been so worried! Are you all right?"

As he nodded, edging through the door with the saddle, she said, "Borden, *please!* You're not going to bring that old saddle into the house!"

"Got to. I want to have it close by." He gestured to it. "This was George Riggin's saddle."

"It's old and it's smelly. Borden, please. Leave it in the stable."

"No, I want to have it close by. Besides, Tom has been wanting a saddle. Maybe I can fix it up for him. He'd like riding the saddle the old marshal rode. Make him the envy of every kid in town."

"You know how I feel about that." She spoke a little sharply. "I don't want that kind of life for Tom, Borden, and you know it. I want him to be a gentleman. A doctor or a lawyer or something of the kind . . . A professional man."

It was an old argument, and he was in no mood for it now. "I think the boy should decide for himself," he said quietly. "Maybe my life hasn't been the best, but I've been a free man, riding wide country under a wide sky. Bess, maybe you don't understand, but I've loved it."

"That was all right for you, but Tom is growing up into another world, a world without all the riding and shooting."

He went on into the bedroom and put the saddle down on the floor. Then with a sigh of relief he lay down, not even taking time to remove his boots, just letting them hang over the edge of the bed.

Needed work, George had told his wife. That was nonsense. George never let anything of his need work. He was a slow-moving man, but meticulous about having everything in shape. When at home he was always sewing on leather, polishing, oiling his guns, repairing whatever needed it.

Borden Chantry closed his eyes and slowly let his long body relax. The bed felt good, and he was tired, so very, very tired.

Suddenly, he was awake. He must have slept for some time, as it was already dark. He lay for a moment, eyes wide, staring up into the darkness and listening . . . What had awakened him?

Bess was in bed beside him. She had simply taken off his boots and let him rest as he was. Slowly, anxious not to awaken her, he sat up, putting his sock feet to the floor. His mouth was very dry and tasted bad, but his head felt better. He got to his feet, and very carefully went through the bedroom door into the short hall.

He paused there, listening. He had no idea what he was listening for, but supposed it might be the sound that had awakened him. Yet perhaps it had been no sound, but simply that he had rested somewhat and as his sleep became lighter his clothes began to bother him. He should just undress and go back to bed.

Yet he was wide awake now. There might be some coffee in the pot and it was a good time to think, to try to put it all together.

As his eyes adjusted to the darkness he decided to light no lamp that might awaken Bess or the boys, but just to get his coffee and sit in the kitchen and think this out, with nothing to hold his attention but his thoughts.

He needed to sit down and clarify the problem. If he could state it clearly, present the arguments pro and con, he might come to a better understanding of what this was all about. The trouble was that he was no great brain, and he needed these times of quiet thought.

The coffeepot was hot. The fire burned slow, but there was a good bed of coals. He lifted the lid on the stove and added a few sticks from the woodbox. Then he took a cup, filled it with coffee, and went to the table.

In his sock feet he made no sound except the slight creak of the floorboards.

Seated in the darkness he once again put together the little he knew.

It left him with a number of questions. What happened to the money the dead man had carried? Why was he in town? What had Johnny known that he intended to tell him? Why did the killer fear identification of the dead man? If Riggin had been murdered, what had he found out that made his death necessary to the murderer?

Pin Dover had been the first to die. Was there any

connection? He drank his coffee and thought about Dover.

A good cowhand, an inoffensive man who got drunk occasionally on paydays and worked hard in-between. Easygoing, friendly, expert with a rope and a good rider. He had worked for a dozen outfits from the Llano to the Pecos, and at least two along the Picketwire.

Suddenly, there was a soft step behind him. Startled, he turned quickly.

Billy McCoy was standing there in one of Tom's old nightshirts. "Mr. Chantry? I just woke up an' remembered somethin'. Then I heard you."

"What is it, Billy?"

"That brand . . . the one on the sorrel? I just remembered. It was either S's or 8's."

"S what? Or 8 what?"

"It was S or 8, I can't be sure which, then a S lyin' down . . . You know, a Lazy S. Then there was another S or 8."

"S-Lazy S-S?"

"I think so. I didn't see it plain, and he hadn't shed all his winter coat. It could have been eights."

"Thanks, Billy. Anything else?"

"Only that Pa was worried about something. He was real worried. Pa was a drinker, you know, an' he never swore off very often. On'y when he had a new job . . . for awhile . . . Or that time him an' Blossom . . ."

"He and Blossom what?"

The boy's face reddened. "Well, Pa an' her, they knowed each other since they was young as me. I think they used to have a case on one another.

"Pa, he saved his money when he was a boy. Blossom, she had a-plenty always. Pa wouldn't marry her without he had money, and he worked to get some. Then he got drunk one time and when he come out of it, he an' her had a quarrel. They busted up.

"Pa got drunk again and when he come out of it he was married to Ma."

"She was a good woman, Billy. A very good woman."

"Yes sir, I know that. And he worked hard after

that, he laid off the booze . . . Ma tol' me all about it
because she heard of it. She knew Blossom . . . They'd
been friends, sort of. Then Ma died and after a spell
he an' Blossom took up where they left off.

"One night he had him a meeting set up to take her
to a dance. He got all fixed up to go out and he
stopped by in Time Reardon's. He run into some fellers
there an' they started buyin' him drinks. Next thing he
knew he passed out, an' somebody else taken Blossom
to the dance. That-there ended it."

"How do you know all this, son?"

"Ma told me some of it then, when Pa was drunk.
Or from fellers around town, I heard it. Then Auntie
Blossom, one day she told me that Pa drank too much.
That I should try to get him to quit.

"He did quit, he was soberin' up to talk to you
and to Blossom. He said that to me. 'I got to do it,
Billy,' he said, 'I got to see Chantry an' tell him what
I know, and then I got to see Blossom.'

" 'You fixin' to marry her, Pa?' I asks him, an' he
said, he didn't think there was much chance of that
now, but he just wanted her to be all right. He said
he had to be sober so's you'd believe him. That nobody'd pay much attention to a drunk, an' he couldn't
blame them."

"Sit down, Billy. You want a glass of milk?"

"No, sir. I am goin' back to bed. It come to me
all of a sudden an' I figured you should know."

"Thanks, Billy. That's the first good break I've had.
It gives me somewhere to start."

"I'll go to bed then."

"Billy? Did you know Pin Dover?"

"Pin? Aw, sure! He worked with Pa, some. Sure,
I knowed him. Boy, was he good with that rope!
Pa said Pin would never amount to nothin' because he
was always driftin'. He never held no job long.

"He got on over to the Bar B with Pa an' was
doin' right well. He was segundo over there, and the
boss liked him. Gave him an up to forty a month, an'
promised him if he stayed on he'd raise him again
. . . An' not many punchers ever got raises.

"Well, you know what he done? He quit. He flat out

quit! He told Pa folks were tryin' to tie him down. Tryin' to get him to buy things, and he said things weighted a man down so's he couldn't travel.

"That was when he taken out for Mora."

"Where?" Borden Chantry caught Billy by the arm. "Did you say Mora? Down in the Santa Fe country?"

"Yes sir. Mora. Pin, he worked for an outfit down there before, an' said he was goin' back."

"You go to bed, Billy." Borden Chantry got to his feet and returned to the bedroom. He had a hunch, and it was a hunch he had to follow now.

Not tomorrow . . . *now*.

Chapter X

Returning to the bedroom he tugged on his boots, then buckled on his gun belt and took up his hat. On second thought he slipped on a jacket as the night was cool.

Frowning, he remembered the sound of whatever it was that had awakened him. Standing in the kitchen, he considered that, then shook his head. No matter. He would walk over to the office now even if it was the middle of the night.

He walked to the kitchen door and stood a moment, looking out into the yard, then toward the barn. The horses were bunched at one side of the corral, heads up, ears pricked. He could barely make them out, but the heads of two of them were against the lighter sky.

Something was bothering them, something close to or inside the barn.

He thought at once of the saddle. It was here, in the house. In the bedroom, in fact.

But no one would be fool enough to come here after a saddle . . . And why the saddle?

He turned suddenly and went to the bedroom. As quietly as could be, he took the saddle from under the bed and ran his fingers over it.

Old George Riggin had never done anything on impulse, nor anything without its reason. If he had left his old saddle to him, there had to be a reason. Borden knew that one of the reasons he had been offered the job of marshal was that Riggin had suggested him for it. He had once told him so, and said that if anything happened to him he wanted Borden to take over.

The old saddle was smooth, polished, in excellent shape considering its years. Suddenly his expert fingers sensed something different. He felt the place again.

On the left side, between the skirt and the stirrup leather, Riggin had made a small pocket, and into it he had slipped a book . . . a tally book such as ranchmen use when keeping a count of cattle on the range or in the stock pens.

Slipping the book out of the pocket, he put it in the inside pocket of his jacket. Going to the drawer, he got out a handkerchief and slipped it into the pocket where the book had been. Now, if somehow the saddle came into the hands of the killer, he might suspect nothing. He might never realize something else had been in that pocket.

Leaving the saddle under the bed, he put on his hat and went to the door. A moment he hesitated, listening into the night, but he heard no sound. Stepping out, he closed the door softly behind him.

Yet this time he did not take his usual path along the south side of the café building to the street, but went behind it and along the north side, emerging in front of the post office. His heels sounded loud in the stillness of the night.

A faint light showed from the café, but that was usual even when the place was locked as it was now. No other lights showed. He walked past the post office and, putting his key in the lock, entered the marshal's office. The jail consisted of four cells behind the office along a corridor.

A light glowed from Kim Baca's cell, and as Borden entered, somebody stirred in the cell nearest the office. The door stood open. Big Injun, gun in hand, was watching him.

"It's all right, Injun," he said gently. "I had to come to the office for something."

He opened the top drawer of the desk and fumbled with several booklets. They were brand books, listing brands from the various states. A couple were printed under the states in question, the others had been put together by George Riggin to enable him to recover stolen stock.

Choosing the book for New Mexico, one of George's own compiling, he ran a finger down a page, then another. On the next to the last page he found it . . .
S-Lazy S-S . . . Sackett.
Sackett!

Shocked, he stared at it. He knew the name well, as did most frontiersmen. The Sacketts were cattlemen in New Mexico and Colorado, a feudal family from Tennessee, if all the stories were right. And if you nudged one Sackett they all woke up.

That was what Reardon had suggested, with no names mentioned.

A Sackett had been murdered . . . or at least a man riding a Sackett horse. If the stories were true, at any moment a troop of them would come along the trail to ask questions, and they were the kind of men who got answers.

Solve the crime and solve it fast. Meet them with the murderer in prison and the evidence gathered.

He grinned sourly. All too easy to say, but how to do it?

"Marshal?" It was Baca calling. "Is that you?"

"Go to sleep, Kim."

"Marshal, I got to talk to you. Besides, I'm not sleepy."

He walked back to find Kim Baca standing at the bars. "When it comes to that, I don't think much of your bunks. The grub's good enough, but those bunks!" He shook his head with disgust.

"Marshal, I sent for you. I want to talk a little, and you'd better listen. I've been thinking about it, and maybe we can help each other."

"No deals. You were caught with the goods, Kim."

"Hell, don't I know it? But look, I'm going to lay it on the line. I'd no intention of stealing that team. I spotted another horse comin' up country . . . a sorrel horse."

Borden walked back to the office and took a spare chair and brought it back. He sat down, straddling the chair and facing the cell. "All right, let's have it."

"Look, I like horses . . . good horses. I spotted that sorrel's tracks coming up the trail and liked that nice swinging stride. Then I saw the horse tied to a hitch rail down the country, just like I said before. I trailed him up the country and when I got a look at the rider I was fit to be tied."

"Well?"

"Marshal, I'm no damn fool. That horse belonged to Joe Sackett. He's a brother to Tell Sackett, an' Tyrel. Remember Tyrel? Who was in that land grant fight down near Mora? Well, he's hell on wheels with a pistol, and his brothers Orrin and Tell are as good or better.

"I wanted that sorrel so bad. Ever' time I saw it I broke into a sweat, but I didn't want it bad enough to steal it from a Sackett.

"Well, it made me so mad to think I'd come all that way trackin' a horse I couldn't have that I just blew my skull and stole that team. I was a damn fool, but better a damn fool than a dead man."

"Kim, was anybody else trailing him?"

"No sir, there wasn't. Believe me, I'd know. He spotted me somehow or other and just dropped off the world there for awhile. I still don't know what he done or how he did it, but Marshal, you're a good man. I'd not like you to have to meet Tell Sackett . . . although it's said they are reasonable, law-abiding men . . . as long as there's law."

"I am the law here, Kim. I'll enforce it."

"Well, now you know."

"Kim, if that man was Joe Sackett, or whoever he was, he was carrying money, a quite a lot of money. Did you see any of it?"

"Sure. He paid cash wherever he went. But you know me, Marshal, I never stole a dime in my life. My trouble is I like better horses than I can afford. I steal horses . . . sure. But I never robbed no man or woman of money. Never rustled a cow, either, other than eatin' beef out on the range."

Borden Chantry studied the young man before him. He had heard a good deal about Kim Baca. He was good with a gun, good enough to need to fear no man, although he was rightfully wary of the Sacketts. He was also a good cowhand when he chose to work, a good trailer, and a rare hand at breaking horses.

The thought of such a man going to prison irritated Chantry, yet that was most certainly where he would go, and he was lucky to get off so easily. Horse stealing was a major offense in a land where a man's life might well depend on his horse, and to take his horse was to leave him to die in a land of such vast expanse and so many enemies.

"You got any idea why Sackett was coming here?"

Baca shook his head. "I got some ideas but they're mostly reasons why he wasn't coming here. He wasn't coming to buy cattle, for instance. He passed some good herds, passed some that would have sold quick for cash.

"He didn't waste any time, either. He came right along, not like he was in any crashing hurry, but not loafing, either. He just kept a-coming.

"There was one thing, though. When he came into town he wasted no time. He went right over to see Mary Ann Haley."

"Do you know her?"

"Naw, I got me a girl friend. Only I know her like ever'body does . . . to say howdy on the street. There was one time when—"

"What?"

"Well, I was only a youngster then . . . seventeen, maybe . . . but I figured I was pretty salty. Maybe I was. Anyway, there was this big miner . . . at least he was a miner when he worked . . . He tried to bully Mary Ann. He wanted money from her. Told her he'd break up her joint and put her out of business unless she paid him.

"One of her girls . . . one I knew from the time she was just a farmer's daughter . . . she told me about it."

"So what happened?"

"I sort of took him aside, and as the Sacketts would say, I read him from the Book. Trouble was, I was only seventeen and he didn't take me serious . . . not at first. I had to straighten him out a little and put him on a trail to California."

"Did he go?"

"Last I saw he was headed right. He wasn't seeing very good but he was on his way."

"Sackett went to see Mary Ann?"

"Well, he went to her house, and they let him in. He wasn't there long . . . not at first. But I figure he knew them. Knew Mary Ann or somebody there because I got a look through a window and he was a-settin' there drinkin' coffee with them."

So the next thing was to see Mary Ann Haley. He got up. "You get some sleep, Baca. If you recall anything else, anything at all, I'd be glad to know."

He hesitated ."You know, Baca, I'm just a sort of a help-out peace officer. I'm not cut out for this job, but although you may not think so, there's got to be law in this country. This man Sackett wasn't killed in any shooting, he was murdered. He was shot from ambush or maybe by somebody he was sitting down with. Anyway, he was shot in the back at close range.

"I've got to get that man, Baca, and I will."

"You don't think it was me?"

"No, I don't. Not unless you got me fooled, but I think you may know more than you think. You've got time to set and think. Well, you go over it. You go over everything that happened, everything you saw or thought you saw, then tell me."

Daylight was just breaking when Chantry got back to the house. He stirred up the fire in the kitchen range and put on water for coffee. He was asleep with his head on his arms on the kitchen table when Bess came in. When she had the coffee made, she shook him awake.

"What happened, Borden? What got you up?"

"I thought I heard somebody in the night. I went out and looked around. Then Billy woke up and remembered something and I went out to the office."

"In the middle of the night?"

"Well, it was important. Bess, Billy remembered the brand on that sorrel horse. I checked it out and the brand belongs to some of the Sackett family."

"I've heard of them. Killers, aren't they?"

"No, Bess, they are not. You'd ride many a mile to find better citizens or men than them Sacketts. They are mountain people from Tennessee, but good folks. They've done some shooting here and there, but this is a hard country, Bess, and it needs hard men to settle it."

"That's why I want to move, Borden. I want to go back east. I want to go to Vermont."

"What would I do there, Bess? I don't know anything but cattle."

"You could farm. You could get some kind of a job."

"Bess," he said patiently, "we've been over this time and again. There's fifty men in this town that used to farm back east and couldn't make it. Now they are here, some of them doing well. I'd never fit in back there, Bess."

"I'm afraid, Borden. I'm afraid you'll be killed. You've been shot at . . . several times. Oh, I know! You didn't tell me about it, but Priss did. Everybody in town is talking about it, and she likes you, you know. She always has."

"I'll be all right. Men never built anything, Bess, without there was some dying and some suffering. I don't want to die. All I want is to be with you and Tom, but I'm doing a job somebody has to do . . . and who else is there?"

"Lang Adams. He's at least single."

"Not for long. He's courtin' Blossom Galey."

"I know. She's a fine woman . . . a little . . . well, she's been around men too much, out on that ranch. She's a little too free-talking. She's just grown up with all those cowboys around."

"Lang could do worse, believe me."

"Borden . . . I wasn't going to tell you, but . . . well, I heard something last night, too."

"When?"

"You were asleep. I heard something, but I didn't get up. Somebody was around the barn, Borden. I lifted the curtain a little and I could just make him out . . . not who it was . . . but it was a man. He went into the barn, then came out. He came up to the back porch and looked through the screen."

"And you didn't call me?"

"Borden, you'd have come out of a deep sleep, and he was already out there in the dark. He'd have had every advantage."

He pushed back from the table and went outside, studying the ground. A few blurred tracks . . . the edge of a boot sole, clean-cut and sharp. In the barn he found a half-inch of a heel track. It was sharply cut . . . New boots, or almost new.

He remembered his one thin clue. Lying on the floor of the mule barn after he had been hit, he had grabbed out and his fingers had slipped off a boot . . . a well-polished boot, that felt almost new.

Borden Chantry walked back into the house, liking the smell of bacon frying. He could hear the boys stirring around in their room as he sat down.

He was going to have to pay attention to boots. He was going to have to find somebody who wore brand-new boots.

And that reminded him that he had to see Hyatt Johnson.

Today.

And he had to see Mary Ann Haley.

When he got up from the table and reached for his hat, Bess turned around, a fork in her hand. "Borden? Be careful."

He walked outside in the bright morning sun and looked toward the McCoy house.

How could he be careful when he had no idea who he had to be careful of?

Somebody in town wanted to kill him. Somebody in town was getting very, very worried.

For somebody time was running out . . . somebody who had shot before, and would again, at any instant.

Chapter XI

It was early for the bank to be open, so after a walk along the street to see if all was well, stopping to speak to Blazer and Elsie, Chantry strolled back to the Bon-Ton, took his usual seat and waited for Ed to bring him coffee.

Two drummers sat in the corner, and a cowboy from west of town was sitting, hat tilted back, dusty spurred boots tucked back under his chair, cooling his coffee in his saucer. He looked to be all of seventeen, but that was a common age for cowhands. In fact, one of the greatest herds ever taken out of Texas to the north had been in charge of a man . . . and he was definitely a man . . . of just seventeen.

Responsibility, like hard work, came very young on the western ranges.

He had scarcely seated himself when Prissy came in. He could see at once that something was worrying her. She looked around quickly and crossed immediately to his table and sat down opposite him. Her eyes were large with excitement.

"Marshal, soon as I saw you on the street I came running. Marshal, you've got to be careful!"

"Well, I try to be, Prissy. What's wrong?"

"Did you ever hear of Boone Silva?"

He felt a sudden emptiness in his stomach. "I have," he said. "Why?"

"Marshal," she leaned closer, "somebody here in town *wrote* to him!"

"They've got the right," he said, "if they know where he lives."

"They knew all right! Marshal, that letter was mailed in one of them cheap kind of envelopes they sell over to the store . . . Ever'body uses them . . . And it was *printed*. The address was printed, like whoever sent it didn't want the handwriting recognized."

"Private business, Prissy. It is none of my affair."

She sat back in her chair. "Isn't it now? Why would anybody from here be sending word to a hired gunman? There's no cattle war on. No trouble of any kind except what you bought for yourself when you began hunting that murderer.

"Somebody shot at you, Marshal. Somebody hit you on the head. Somebody killed poor Johnny McCoy. I think when you got George Riggin's saddle—"

"How did you know about that?" he demanded sharply.

"Marshal, you've lived here long enough. Nobody has any secrets in this town. Mrs. Riggin told Elsie that George wanted you to have his saddle . . . Now why would you want another saddle? If he was going to give it to somebody why not little Billy McCoy, who got his bridle? Ever'body just naturally figures there had to be some *reason*. You know, that maybe George was tryin' to *tell* you something.

"Well, when I saw that letter to Boone Silva, I just *knew* it was account of you. Somebody wants you dead, Marshal, somebody wants you dead almighty bad. Now you just watch. In a few days he'll come ridin' into town, and—"

"You sent the letter?"

"Had to. It's my bounden duty. All the same, you being the Law, I figured you should ought to know."

"Thanks, Prissy." He filled his cup. Then he thought of the obvious question. "Where did the letter go to, Prissy?"

"Trinidad." He filled her own cup. "Marshal, it makes a body wonder. How did whoever wrote that letter know where to find him? The way I heard it, Silva was around Tascosa, and if not there, Las Vegas. How did whoever wrote that letter know to write him in Trinidad?"

It was a good question, a very good question. Borden Chantry stared into his cup. God, he thought, don't let Bess hear about this!

Silva was a gunfighter . . . He'd been an outlaw, had done time in prison, and lately had been riding for various ranches around the country, driving nesters off

the land. He had killed three or four men in gun battles, and it was said a half-dozen more should be
added to the list, but who knew about that?

"Don't say anything about this, Prissy," he warned.
Yet even as he said it he knew what a talker she was,
and doubted she could keep the story even if she tried.

Her next comment reassured him. "Don't worry.
You think I want that man to know I told you *that?*
He might decide to kill me. I just won't tell anybody,
Marshal, and don't you, neither."

She got up and left just as Blossom Galey came into
the room. She saw him at once, and crossed to his table. "Hi, Bord! It's good to see you! Seen Lang this
morning?"

"No, I haven't. Sit down, Blossom. I've been mean-
ing to ride out your way."

"Now, Bord, you know better than that! Why, you're
a married man with a family!"

He blushed, and she laughed, delighted.

"I didn't mean that," he protested, "I just wanted
to talk to you about George Riggin."

"George?" Her face saddened. "That was bad, real
bad! I liked old George. He was a real man. Don't
find his kind around much any more." Then she looked
at him. "What about him, Borden? If there's anything
I can help you with, you just let me know."

"He was coming out to see you when he was killed.
Had you sent for him?"

"Me? I should say not! Why would I need the law?
If anybody gave me any trouble, I've got a Winchester.
That's all the law I need on my land, because if anybody was troubling me it would be rustlers, and I'd
take care of that myself, just like Pa used to."

"Better leave it to the law, Blossom."

"What law? You're the *town* marshal. You've got
no jurisdiction out yonder. We've got us a county
sheriff I hear, but I've never seen him. Maybe there's a
United States marshal in Denver, but how does that
help me? By the time I got to him and he got here my
cows would be in Mexico."

"He wanted to talk to you, Blossom. Have you got
any idea what it was about?"

She hesitated . . . just a moment too long. "No, not really, Borden. George was like a second father to me, in some ways. He was a good man, but he never trusted anybody very much, and he was always afraid I'd get into trouble."

"You don't know why he suddenly decided he had to see you?"

"No," she said again, more quickly this time.

He did not persist, yet the idea remained that she did know why George Riggin had been coming to see her, or had an idea. Why, then, would she not tell him?

For a moment his thoughts returned to Boone Silva. The man was notoriously fast with a gun, and a dead shot. Suppose Priscilla was right and he was being sent for to kill him? How would he stack up with Silva? He had never considered himself a gunfighter, and had dodged any suggestion of the kind. He was good with a gun, but he'd never had any idea of matching skills with anyone . . . this was for crazy kids. He had no idea of killing anyone.

Yet supposing he was faced with it? Right here on the street?

He shook his head to clear away the thought. He would straddle that bronc when time put a saddle on it. For now, he had too much else to do.

"You don't mind if I sit here?" Blossom asked suddenly. "I'm waiting for Lang."

"Sorry, I was wool-gathering. Got a lot to think about these days."

Who would know about Silva? Kim Baca, of course. Kim knew all the men who followed the outlaw trail.

He got up suddenly. "Blossom? Stick around, will you? I want to talk to you again. I've got to run up to the bank now."

"Oh, I'll be in town! There's a dance . . . or didn't you know? Lang's taking me."

He'd better talk to Bess. She liked dancing. And oddly enough, for a man who was not very social, he liked it, too. And they all said he was good. Well . . . maybe.

He walked up the street, watching people from habit.

At the bank he turned and looked down the street again. Supposing somebody had sent for Silva to kill him? Would Silva be likely to shoot from ambush? Or face him somewhere?

If Kim Baca did not know, Time Reardon might. Would he get an honest answer from Time? He considered that, and decided he would. Time would tell him, no matter how it was. Well, that was what he wanted.

He entered the bank and the teller motioned with his head toward Johnson's office. The banker looked up as Chantry came in.

"Ah? How are you, Chantry? Sorry I was so short with you the other day, but I am rather jealous of my files. People like to keep their financial affairs a secret, you know, so I hesitated."

"What did Sackett want?"

Hyatt hesitated only for a minute. "He opened an account. He gave me a check for three thousand dollars on a bank in Santa Fe."

"Three thousand?" Chantry dropped into a chair. "Did he give you any idea why he was depositing it?"

"As a matter of fact, he did." Hyatt Johnson sat back in his swivel chair. "It must be confidential, of course. He was anxious that she know nothing about it until he had done some checking. He wanted to see if there was any man around who might be taking money from her."

"Her?"

"Mary Ann Haley."

They stared at each other, and then Johnson shook his head. "It isn't what you might think. Sackett explained it very quickly, very simply.

"A few years ago there was an epidemic in a western mining camp. Mary Ann Haley, risking her own health, nursed a number of men through their illness, and one of them was a Sackett.

"Well, you've heard about the Sacketts. They pay their debts. Somebody came through Mora and happened to tell them that Mary Ann was sick, that she needed to change her climate, but didn't have the money.

"That was all they needed to know. Several Sacketts put up money and Joe started over the trail, part of it in cash, and the rest in a draft on that bank in Santa Fe.

"He went to see her, but he wasn't satisfied. You know how it is. Often those girls are keeping some man on the side who simply takes all their money, and Joe wanted to look into the situation before he gave her the rest of the money. He also wanted to make up his mind whether she should have it all, or just a drawing account.

"He deposited the check with me, and he left his saddlebags."

"Saddlebags?"

Hyatt Johnson turned toward the big safe. It was an old safe, no longer used for the day-to-day banking business, but as a place of safekeeping for valuables of local people or travelers.

Opening the safe, he took out a pair of worn saddlebags and dropped them on the desk. "You'll have to sign for them, Marshal. It isn't that I do not trust you, but they were left to me for safekeeping."

"Sure. I'll sign." Borden Chantry got to his feet. "Thanks, Hyatt. This is a help. Now, for the first time, I really know why he came to town. It helps."

Hyatt pushed a sheet of paper to him, and Borden signed. As he was signing his name, Hyatt added, "Marshal, Sackett was carrying gold, a good deal of it."

"How much?"

Johnson shrugged. "Several hundred dollars . . . maybe more. It was in a money belt and a sack he had tucked under his coat. It was heavy . . . I could tell from the way he moved."

"Thanks." Johnson sat back in his chair again, and Chantry moved to the door of the office. "I'll talk to Mary Ann."

Hyatt Johnson shifted in his chair. "Chantry? I'd be careful. Be damned careful. They've missed up until now, when they try for you, but they didn't miss with Johnny McCoy or with Sackett."

His route down the street took him past the Corral Saloon. He paused in the door, then went in. Two men

were playing cards at one of the tables, and a freighter
was at the bar with a beer.

Time Reardon was polishing a glass when Chantry
came in, and he put it down and walked to the far
end of the bar to meet him. He took the cigar from his
teeth. "Something for you, Marshal?"

"A little conversation," Chantry rested his thick fore-
arms on the edge of the bar. "What do you know about
Boone Silva?"

Reardon took the cigar from his teeth. "I have
never done any business with him," he said slowly,
"but the word is that he's a dangerous man."

"Would he kill a man for hire?"

Reardon smiled. "He'd kill a man for hire, he'd kill
a man for fun, and he might just kill him to get him
out of the way. The man's completely without con-
science or scruples, Chantry, and anybody who deals
with him is begging for trouble.

"He's a man of about five nine or ten. Weighs about
one sixty, I'd say. He's a dark, swarthy man with
black hair but pale blue eyes . . . kind of a glassy look
to them. The top of one of his ears is cut cleanly off
. . . I don't know how . . . but he usually keeps it covered with hair.

"He's good with any kind of a gun, and he'll shoot
you from the front or the back."

"That's what I wanted to know . . . what to expect."

Reardon took up his cigar. "Whiskey?" he suggested.

"I'll have a beer."

Reardon poured himself a drink. "Rarely touch the
stuff," he said frankly. "It doesn't mix well with business . . . or guns. Or cards."

He took a bottle from under the bar and a glass.
He filled the glass with beer. "Is he coming here? After
you?"

"I don't know, but there's a suggestion that he
might." Chantry tasted the beer. "Reardon, I don't
know much about such things. What would it cost to
hire a man like that?"

Reardon smiled, then shrugged. "Marshal, Silva
would kill a sheepherder or a cook or a drifter for fifty

dollars. For a nester it would cost a hundred . . . **if he** had a family."

"For me?"

"Two hundred . . . maybe more. There are some who say you are very good with a gun yourself. He'd want at least two hundred, and he'd want the odds." Reardon dusted the ashes from his cigar. "He'd want you armed, so he would have an excuse, but he'd try to pick a time when you weren't ready. Suppose you've been having coffee over at the Bon-Ton, and you start to rise from the table. Often a man will rest a hand on the table or a chair in rising, or you grasp the pommel of your saddle, preparing to mount . . . He'll pick a time that works for him, Marshal, and he won't miss."

"Two hundred? That's a fair chunk of money."

"It is that." Reardon smiled but his eyes were cold. "Not many men in town could ante up that kind of money. I suspect Johnson could. Blazer might. Blossom Galey could."

"Why Blossom?"

"She's got money enough. Whether she has the reason, I wouldn't know. If I were you, Marshal, I'd not rule anybody out who could pay two hundred dollars."

"Including you?"

Reardon chuckled. "Including me." He looked straight into Chantry's eyes. "But that's a lot of money to spend, Marshal, when I own a Winchester."

"You left somebody out," Chantry said.

"Who?"

"Mary Ann Haley," he said, and drank the last of his beer.

Chapter XII

Borden Chantry walked south on Main Street until he was past the Mexican café, then turned along the well-worn path toward Mary Ann's house, which stood back by itself in a small grove of trees.

It was a square white house on which a small addition had been added, a porch across the front, shaded by several big old cottonwoods. There was a stable in back and a hitching rail in front. He saw no horses as he approached, no sign of life other than a thin trail of smoke from the chimney.

He paused in the shade of the nearest cottonwood. There was a slight breeze there and it felt cool. He removed his hat and wiped his hatband. He did not like what he had to do. Questioning women was something he would never like, and especially as Mary Ann was sick.

Was she a suspect? Sackett had been to her house, and he had been carrying considerable money. He had brought the money for her, and had more waiting in the bank, but did she know that?

Mary Ann had no boyfriend hanging around. If she had, everybody in town would have known it. Lucy Marie now, she was sweet on one of the riders out at the O-Bar-O, sometimes called the Dumbbell. Chantry went up the steps, spurs jingling a little. The boards creaked under his weight. He tapped on the door.

It opened at once, almost as if he had been expected. Lucy Marie answered the door.

"Marshal? Won't you come in?"

He stepped in, removing his hat. "How are you, Lucy? Is Mary Ann in?"

"You come and sit down, Marshal. I'll go tell Mary Ann you're here."

As she left the room, he glanced around. It might

have been any parlor in any house in town, except there was a piano, and he knew of only one other in town. And that was in the church. No, that was an organ.

The carpets were a little thicker. The furniture was velvet or something that looked like it. There was a lot of red . . . and it was a little brighter than he'd expect to find in most houses.

The curtains parted and he looked around at Mary Ann Haley, rising to his feet as she entered. "How do you do?" he said. "I'm sorry to disturb you."

"It is all right, Marshal. I feel a little better today."

"I am investigating the murder of Joe Sackett."

"So I assumed. Do you want to know what I know about him? Or is it something else?"

Before he could reply, she turned her head. "Lucy? Make us some tea, will you?" She glanced at him. She was a pale, quite lovely woman, he decided. And on this day she wore a gingham dress in blue and white with a square-cut collar with some lace around it, and on the cuffs. He wasn't much good at such things, but he looked because he knew Bess would be curious. Disapproving, but curious.

"You do drink tea, don't you, Marshal?"

"Anything. Oh, sure. But you needn't bother."

"It's quite all right."

She was visibly thinner than when he had last seen her, and she had always given the impression of being frail—unusual in women of her kind in this part of the country. And she was no youngster . . . Forty? Maybe. And maybe younger, for she'd had quite a life. He remembered patches of stories he'd heard here and there.

Her folks had been killed by Indians nearly thirty years back, and she had been taken up by foster parents who'd been none too good to her. She'd run off, joined a traveling show, had married an actor who ran off and left her when she grew ill. She had been in California, then Nevada . . . That was where she had stuck by the boys when they got sick, and risked her life to help them through their illness.

She'd been known in Virginia City, Pioche, Leadville, and Tin Cup, and some said she had worked the cattle towns further east.

Somewhere along the line she had taken up with a gambler, but he had been killed when a stage overturned. Since then there had been nobody.

"You wanted to ask about Joe Sackett. I had never met him until he rode into town. One of his brothers was ill out west and I helped nurse him to health, along with some other men. He heard I was in trouble, and Joe came to bring me some money."

"How much?"

"Five hundred dollars . . . to start. They said there would be more when I got located out on the coast."

"Joe Sackett gave you five hundred dollars. Do you know how much more he had?"

"I've no idea, but he did have more. I saw it."

"Was there anybody else here that night?"

"It was morning when he first came, but I wasn't awake yet. He came back later. He explained why he had come and that his brother and several others had contributed. They said I had helped them, they wished to help me. I was to take the money and go to San Diego, where another one of the miners I helped had a house in which I could live. The climate would be right for me, and the money would care for me."

"Pretty nice," Chantry said. "Did you talk about anything else?"

"Well, he asked about the town and the people. He did say something to the effect that he'd seen a man on the street whom he thought he remembered from New Mexico."

"Did he describe him?"

"Oh, no! And I thought nothing of it because a lot of the men from here have been down there. Some of the cowhands from the ranches try to work further south when cold weather comes. Can't blame them. It's cold out on that range."

"Don't I know?" Chantry agreed, grimly.

Lucy brought the tea and sat quietly.

He sipped his tea, while she talked of western mining camps, and the hard times. What did he know, after all? That Joe Sackett had come to town to help Mary Ann. That he had given her some money, that he had deposited more in the bank, and that he had left. He had been assaulted by Kerns and Hurley, had taken care of them, but had never arrived at the hotel.

Somebody had shot him in the back . . . but where? Sackett had his coat off at the time . . . why?

Sackett was no tenderfoot, so how had somebody come up behind him? Was it somebody he knew and trusted?

"Was there anybody else here at the time?"

"There was nobody here in the morning," she said thoughtfully. "Not when he came, at least. And when he came back?" She paused, thinking. "Well . . . I've forgotten. There were several here, not for business, just dropping in to visit or have a drink."

"Do you know Boone Silva?" he asked suddenly. Her expression did not change.

She shrugged one slender shoulder. "I've heard of him."

"The second time he was here," he suggested. "I mean Sackett. What time did he leave?"

She had the cup almost to her lips but she stopped and put it down. "Why, I don't remember! He was here, and he was reading a magazine he picked up. I had grown tired so I went up to bed. Maybe Lucy can tell you."

Lucy shook her head. "Yes, he was here. He read the paper and drank some coffee."

"Nothing else?"

"No, I don't think he drank. Coffee was all he had. After he read the paper he went to wash his hands, and then came back. And right after that, he left."

"Did he say where he was going? What he was going to do?"

"Mary Ann offered him a room here." She looked up at Chantry. "We have extra rooms. Sometimes people we know do stay over, and sometimes when somebody has too much to drink, we put them in one of the spare rooms. But he said he would go to the hotel." She paused, suddenly frowning. "You know, when he left . . . I thought maybe he wasn't feeling well. I asked him again to stay, but he just shook his head and went on. Once I thought he was going to fall, and I started toward him, but he straightened up and went on."

On? To where?

Some had said he was staggering, looking like he might be drunk. But he drank little, if at all.

He had only coffee.

"Lucy Marie? I want you to think. Who made the coffee?"

"Why, I did. I usually do, although once in awhile Mary Ann would."

Doped coffee? For what purpose? He had already given them money, and planned to give Mary Ann more. Lucy Marie? He looked at her thoughtfully. Lucy Marie and somebody else, trying for a little money on their own?

He doubted it. Yet the thought was there.

"Was Blazer in here that night? I need witnesses," he said then. "Somebody who can tell me where Sackett was going, what he planned to do."

Mary Ann spoke reluctantly. "What men do who come here is their own business, and I don't want to know or ask questions unless they feel like talking. Some of them are lonely, and they just want to talk. We're used to that. Some of the cowboys never see a woman for months at a time and when they come in they want to talk. They're just lonely, as much as anything.

"Yes, Mr. Blazer was here, but so was Hyatt Johnson and Lang Adams. They were just sort of making the rounds, I guess."

"Time Reardon came by, too," Lucy Marie commented, "but he didn't stay long. He was looking for somebody, I think."

Borden Chantry finished his tea. He put the cup down carefully. It was elegant china, and he tried to identify the pattern so he could tell Bess about it.

"That coffee," he said, "were you alone in the kitchen when you made it?"

"Oh, Lord no!" Lucy Marie laughed. "That kitchen

is the busiest room in the house. There's always some-body coming or going."

He stayed a little longer, asked a few more questions, and wished he could think of something to ask that might uncover some information he could use. But he was no good at questions. Still, he had an idea there had been something in that coffee, for Sackett seemed to have been affected soon after drinking it. There seemed to be no reason why either of the girls would have doped his coffee . . . Yet something happened to Sackett, something that left him staggering and uncertain after leaving Mary Ann's.

At the door he said good-bye, put on his hat and drew the door shut behind him. For an instant, he stood there, his eyes sweeping the terrain before him, then he moved into the shade of the nearest cottonwood and stood again.

Where had Sackett been going when he left Mary Ann's? Logic said the hotel. He had left his horse earlier at McCoy's. He had no reason to go anywhere except the hotel or perhaps to the Mexican café or the Bon-Ton to eat. Supposedly, he was a stranger in town.

Had he met somebody at Mary Ann's? There'd been no mention of it, yet it could have happened. Had he encountered someone after leaving Mary Ann's?

Looking due north, and some three hundred yards away, was the old freight barn where Chantry had been rapped on the skull. Less than a hundred yards off, the Mexican café. And across the street and just a bit farther, the McCoy place. His own place was about three hundred yards to the northwest, and mostly west, so as he walked away he began to retrace the steps Sackett had taken.

It was sandy, weed-covered ground with a few scattered patches of prickly pear. Near the Mexican café there were a couple of trees, and his own house stood in a cluster of them.

Supposing . . . just supposing, Sackett had been hot? Supposing he had himself removed his coat, carrying it over his arm?

Supposing also that instead of going directly to the street west of Mary Ann's, he had gone northwest past the back of the Mexican café?

The Corral Saloon, except for the door at the rear, had a blank wall. The old freight barn was empty and deserted. There would have been a moment there when Sackett was not in the view of anybody.

There was no use looking for tracks at this late date, for aside from the element of time, numerous dogs, children and occasional horses or cattle had walked or been driven over the area in passing from one place to another.

Another thought came to him. The arroyo in which he had found the saddle was only a little way off to the east.

Again he came back to the thought of motive. Someone with a hate for the Sackett family? The desire for the gold he carried?

Yet how could that fit into the killing of Pin Dover, and of George Riggin—if he was killed . . . and of Johnny McCoy?

Or was there any connection at all? Riggin had believed Dover's death was murder . . . why? And Dover had been punching cows in the Mora area where Sackett came from. It was a feeble connection, but at least a connection.

He started suddenly toward the freight barn. Yet when he had taken no more than a dozen steps, he turned sharply left and in a few steps had the Mexican café between himself and the town.

He went on home.

Bess was sewing when he came into the house. She looked up. "Are you all right?"

"Sure," he said, "a mite tired, is all." He dropped into a chair, putting his hat on the table, his spurs jingling as he moved his boots to an easier position. "Saw Mary Ann."

Bess looked up. "How is she?"

"Frail," he said. "Frail. Sackett was bringing her money. Enough so's she could go out to the coast. Seems a lot of the miners she nursed through that epidemic think highly of her."

He described her appearance as best he could, and told of the parlor and its furniture, the few pictures, and whatever he could remember.

"I don't see what all you men see in her," Bess said stiffly. "She's really not very pretty, and she's so *thin*."

"Well, she's sick. But it isn't only her, Bess. Some of the men go there because it's a place to meet, and she has the latest newspapers there. Why, she's got more papers than I knew was published, and magazines, too."

He tipped back in his chair. "Damned if I can make head or tail of it, Bess. I guess I'm just not cut out for this job."

"Why bother? The man's dead, isn't he? You can't bring him back. Maybe he needed killing."

"A man who would ride a couple of hundred miles to bring money to a sick woman? No, he didn't need killing, but somebody thought he did.

"I don't think it was the money. I think somebody was scared."

"What about Kim Baca? You told me that he'd admitted planning to steal Sackett's horse."

"Right. But he's a horse thief, not a killer. Not that he couldn't if he had to. He's faster than most."

What he should do, he reflected, was get a tablet and write it all out. Who his suspects were, what there was to make him suspect each, and where they were at the times of the shootings.

Suddenly, he flushed, embarrassed that he had not thought of that. Where, for example, had each of them been when Johnny was shot? When he was slugged?

He was a fool. Old George Riggin would have been smarter than that.

Riggin . . . only then did he remember the thin notebook he had taken from the hidden saddle pocket.

It might hold all the answers.

Chapter XIII

He said nothing about the book. It was the usual little notebook, the sort many ranchers called a tally book, and in which they kept count of cattle out on the range, or notes on range conditions. Most men carried such things in their heads, but if you ran a lot of stock such a tally book was handy.

Supposing George had actually named a name? Supposing that book held the solution to the crimes? Was that what he wanted? Or was he afraid of what he might find there? After all, he knew everybody in town, was friendly with them all, even Time Reardon ... And the killer had to be one of them.

He turned it over in his mind, sorting out the little he had learned, trying to find a pattern.

The killer, he thought then, would be nervous. The killer knew him although he did not know the killer, and the killer would be watching his every step, seeing when he got close, laughing when he drifted away from the truth. Yet there was another point to be considered. The killer might be getting nervous.

What was the old saying? *The guilty flee when no man pursueth?* Supposing the killer believed he was closer to a solution than he was? Of course, that had already happened, for the killer had tried to kill him ... or warn him off.

The boys came in for supper and he glanced at Billy, who hastily averted his eyes. Now what was the matter with him? Acted as if he was guilty of something, but that was silly. Next thing, he'd be suspecting Bess ... or Tom.

There was much talk as usual, but his mind was elsewhere. His thoughts reverted to Boone Silva. Silva could be riding into town any time in the next few days, and he would choose his time carefully. Borden

Chantry had one small advantage . . . Boone Silva would not realize that he was expected.

It might make all the difference in the world.

When supper was over he watched the boys help Bess wash and dry the dishes, then he took a cup of coffee and went into the parlor.

Bess looked around in surprise when he opened the door, for the parlor was rarely used except to receive the preacher or some other notable, but tonight he wanted to be alone.

"I've got to study on this," he said.

"Of course," she agreed. It was not the quietest place with the boys around, but he enjoyed their presence nonetheless.

As he went through the door he picked up Sackett's saddlebags. Seated on the sofa, he rested them between his feet and unbuckled the straps.

He hesitated a moment, some inner delicacy making him uncomfortable at thus invading the privacy of another man's belongings. He was himself an essentially private man, friendly but reserved, standing a cool sentry before the doors of his personal life. He had equal respect for the privacy of others.

Suddenly, his hands froze where they were. That strap . . . the one he had just unbuckled . . . had been fastened in the next to the loosest hole, and that wasn't logical. A man carrying anything in saddlebags would cinch them tight so nothing would be lost. Yet if someone had gone into the bags, and had been in a hurry to strap them up, they might have been left just so.

He shook his head irritably. Who around here would do a thing like that? Bess . . . certainly not. Tom? No. Billy? He thought about that. No, Billy was an honest boy and he knew him as such. There had been countless times when Billy might have picked up something around town, but he never had.

He reached into the saddlebag and took out a small sack of .44's, a square of pemmican and a small sack of cold flour, an emergency ration often carried on the trail in earlier days. There was a tight coil of rawhide string, perhaps ten or twelve feet of it, such as a man might carry for rigging snares, use as piggin strings, or a variety of ways around a camp fire or on the range. It was something handy to have, often useful.

In the other bag there was little else. A spare bandana, a small packet of letters, some writing materials, and some odds and ends that might have been carried by any man riding across country.

The letters, all but one, were addressed to *Joe Sackett*. That one was addressed to *Tyrel Sackett*.

Two were from a girl in Santa Fe, the very formal letters of the time, yet betraying a deep interest . . . The first was obviously a love letter. The second was almost identical to the first in tone, telling the small happenings of every day, urging him to come for a visit, and expressing anxiety about his "trip," obviously this one, from which Joe Sackett would not return.

There was a quiet sweetness in the letters that was touching, despite the formal language.

Borden swore softly, bitterly. Somebody would have to write to her, and he thanked the Good Lord it would not have to be him. When a man was killed the circle of ripples on the pool widened to affect many others than himself. It would seem so light a thing, the death of one man, yet who knew how wide the effect might be?

The letter addressed to Tyrel Sackett was simple enough.

Deer Ty:
    Met a feller name of Heine Kellerman. Used to prospect around. He wos inn camp the time the cholery used up the boys an Mary Ann Haley stood by us all, nursin us throo it. Tells me she's down eastern Colo. way, almighty sick with lung-fever. Him an some of the boys done collected muny to send her. Figgered youd be wishful of puttin in an seein it taken to her.
    Con Fletcher is riden down from Leadville with sum more muny in his poke.

                                            Cap Rountree

That must have been the letter that began it all. Or, at least, began Sackett's part in it. Whatever was going on—if there actually was a connection—had started before that, with the death of Pin Dover. Yet why was *he* killed? Maybe for something even before that.

Returning the letters to the saddlebags he strapped them up again. Nothing there, except that he might have had an identification right off if Hyatt had given them up, for Joe Sackett's name was here, in several places.

The worst of it was, he no longer had any excuse for not notifying the Sackett family. Their address was now in his hands. The identification was positive.

Once notified, the Sacketts could be here within four or five days, maybe a bit longer, and he had no solution to lay in their laps.

They had a reputation for strict honesty, but for being hard-nosed about one of their own being killed. And he wanted no interference until he had something to offer.

George Riggin had been killed when he seemed to have reached a conclusion, or was close to one. He got up suddenly and drew tight the curtains. Then he sat down and took out Riggin's tally book.

On the first page, obviously an old list, were some brands and the number of head found with each. They were out-of-state brands, and evidently a count of cattle picked up on the range, found with rustlers or something of the sort. There was on the next few pages a day-to-day arrest records for drunks, brawls, domestic squabbles and the like. It was routine stuff.

On the fourth page: *DOVER, PIN, Investigation of Murder.*

No known enemies . . . Deceased had two dollars in his pocket . . . no known criminal associations. Reputation for honesty. Good average hand. Has a woman in Trinidad, going on eight years. No gambling losses or wins of more than a few cents in several years. Jealousy, robbery, and enemies ruled out. No rustling in area. His horse wasn't taken. No tracks near body. Saturday night drinker. Good-natured drunk. Local work; worked two summers for Borden Chantry, three for Blossom Galey. Employed by Blossom Galey at

*time of killing. Last previous job in Mora for S-Lazy
S-S.*

The Sackett brand . . . there was the tie-up, but
what did it mean? Joe Sackett had come to town on a
simple, peaceful mission. Pin Dover had quit one job
in Mora, ridden north, and gone to work on a place
where he had worked before, and probably within the
past few months or over the years many a cowhand had
done just that. It was the very pattern of existence for
them.

Shortly after his return he had been shot.

Borden Chantry shook his head, then went back to
the tally book, keeping his place with a finger on the
line he was reading.

*Maybe: Pin Dover was killed because of something
he had done . . . something he knew . . . something he
had seen.*

*Maybe: something seen or known about somebody
here? Worry absent when he was gone? Worry increased when he returned?*

Or something he learned while he was gone?

*Ed Pearson had prospected near Mora; he once
herded sheep near Mora. Pin Dover punched cows at
Mora.*

*Hyatt Johnson said to have been implicated in Land
Grant fights at Mora . . . this only rumor . . . No evidence so far.*

No connection between Blossom Galey and Mora.

*Dover's body found where old trail crosses Two
Butte Creek. Position of killer found 150 yds to n.w.
Small knoll, some brush. Timbered area, good for escape, close behind. Fnd. cartridge shell .52 calibre
in rabbit-brush nearby. Some evidence killer searched
for same.*

*Crispin metallic cartridge shell . . . used by some
units in War Between the States.*

*Know of no such rifle or cartridge in area. Used in
Gilbert Smith weapon.*

Chantry put the book down on the sofa beside him,
and sat back to think. Methodically, he went over
every detail of the killings. His was a careful mind. He
had never considered himself an intellect, just a com-

mon-sense sort of man, and that was his only approach. He owned no special knowledge, no remarkable skills. He hoped, by continually re-examining the few odds and ends, that somehow a pattern would emerge. He knew enough of tracking both men and animals to know that most conform to a pattern . . . that few have originality or deviate from accustomed paths. A deer, for example, will rarely stray more than a mile from the place of its birth.

The murderer seemed to be a local man, with local knowledge, and he had to work within the framework of that knowledge. And if there was a cause for killing, it must spring from some source that was locally inspired, or that might affect him . . . or her . . . locally.

Hyatt had attempted to withhold information. He also had been in a position from which he could have killed Johnny McCoy.

Was there any connection between Pin Dover and Hyatt? Between Pin Dover and Blossom Galey, beyond that he was working for her?

Who had been in the barn that night aside from the murderer and himself?

Who owned a rifle of a kind to use that .52 calibre cartridge?

In occasional hunts and turkey shoots, Borden was sure he had seen every rifle in the area, but could recall no such gun.

George Riggin had not told anyone about the .52-calibre rifle, and Chantry decided to do the same. It was a clue . . . although a flimsy one.

The only person he could think of as likely to have such a rifle was Ed Pearson.

A thought came to him suddenly that should have occurred at once. The rifle that fired the shots at him had not had the heavy boom of a .52, but of a lighter, more modern weapon. So the murderer had more than one rifle.

That was not unusual, for nearly every ranch house within miles had two or more rifles and probably a shotgun, to say nothing of the houses here in town. It was the custom of the country, developed from the need to hunt for food and protect the hearth and home, but also from the feeling that freedom won with the gun might have to be kept with the gun. Here, as in Switzerland, the militia was the people.

Mora . . . it all came back to Mora. Yet might that not be a blind alley? That might be pure coincidence.

He had surmised the killer was a local man, working from local knowledge. He was also sure that something he had done had worried or frightened the killer into attempting to kill *him*. It might have been the discovery of the brand on the dead horse that started it, but it was evidence enough that the killer was watching.

So why not give him something to watch? Why not offer the killer some bait and draw him from under cover? Suppose Chantry let word get around that he had a source of information, and then he saddled up and rode out? Would he be followed? And if he was followed, would that not be first-rate evidence as to the killer?

Yet that meant setting himself up as a target, deliberately putting himself in the way of being shot at, perhaps killed.

He got up, put the tally book in his pocket and started back downtown. Bess called after him, and he turned. She stood in the door, staring after him. "Borden? Will you be long?"

"Not long. I have to talk to somebody."

He went into the jail and nodded to Big Injun, then opened the door to the space where the cells were. Kim Baca came to the bars. "How long am I going to be locked up here?" he demanded. "If they're going to try me, why wait?"

"The judge will be along. He's comin' this way." Borden put his hands on the bars. "Kim, how much of a man are you?"

"What?" The outlaw's face flushed. "What kind of talk is that? I'm as good as any damn man, an' I'll have you—"

"Is your word any good? I've heard that it was."

Kim stared at him, puzzled and wary. "My word's good. I never broke my word for anybody."

"Kim, we've got an open an' shut case against you.

We can send you over the road with no trouble. You know that, don't you?"

"I'll get me a good lawyer."

"It won't help much, but you could help yourself by helping me. If you were to help me, my word to the judge might carry weight."

"What kind of help?"

"I'm going to have to leave town, Kim. Somebody in town wants to kill me. When I go, I want you to watch and see who follows me, at least who leaves town."

"How can I watch from in here? I can't see much from that window."

"Didn't figure you could. You're going to give me your word that you won't try to escape, and I'm going to turn you loose."

"You're *what?*"

"I'm going to put you on what they call parole. You can set around outside, eat in the café, have yourself a drink, but you can't leave town. All you've got to do is see who rides out of town and keep your mouth shut."

"You'd trust me? Why, Marshal, I'm just liable to steal one of your own horses and ride out of here. That Appaloosa of yours, now—"

"I'll be ridin' him."

"Well, one of the others, then. How do you know I won't do that?"

"I don't. But I'm bettin' you're a man of your word." Borden Chantry put the key in the lock and opened the cell door. "Come on out, Baca. An' just to let folks know you've a right to be out, I'm walking down to the Bon-Ton to buy you a cup of coffee."

Chapter XIV

Lang Adams was seated near the window when they walked in, and Prissy was at a table with Elsie. Hyatt Johnson was at another window table, and all looked up when Borden Chantry walked in with Kim Baca.

"Well!" Lang looked from one to the other, smiling. "This is a surprise."

"Big Injun won't be around today," Borden said mildly, "so Baca gave me his parole and he'll be around town."

"Taking a chance, aren't you?" Lang suggested. "I wouldn't blame Baca if he grabbed another horse and left the country."

"He won't do it," Borden sat down and glanced around. Hyatt was watching him, cup poised. Listening, too. "Baca gave me his word, and I believe in him."

Kim Baca shrugged, and glanced at Adams. "He's a trustin' sort, and there aren't too many left. He still believes in folks, trusts in a man's word. Why, I do believe he'd hire me to care for his horses!"

Chantry turned his eyes to Baca. "Want the job?" he asked gently. "I could use a good man."

Lang Adams shrugged. "Baca, you'll find Chantry that kind of man, but whatever you do, don't cross him. If you ever ran out on him he'd follow you until he died . . . or you did. He's like a bulldog . . . never knows when to let go."

Conversation picked up and Borden looked out into the night and thought of his next move. He did need Big Injun, and there would have been nobody to care for Baca in jail. Also, he could use Baca.

Secretly, he knew there was yet another reason. Deep inside he was sure Kim Baca was a good man, a better man than most, yet with a taste for expensive horseflesh and not the money to buy it. Yet given a chance,

114

Baca might become any kind of man he wished to be, and Chantry disliked seeing him go to prison where his future would be twisted the wrong way. Given this chance, he might make good. And if so, Borden would do as he promised and speak for him to the judge, a man he knew well as a hard-nosed frontiersman.

The judge believed in stiff penalties, but he was a man of much experience with the world and aware that all are prone to make mistakes. He would, Borden believed, give Kim Baca a chance. He would also sentence him to hang if he failed to make good. He was that kind of man, harsh yet understanding.

Lang Adams was quiet. He talked a little, and when Borden asked him about Blossom Galey, Lang shot a glance at Baca and did not reply for several minutes. "She's all right," he said at last. "Shorthanded right now, so I may go help her."

"She lost a good hand in Pin Dover," Chantry agreed. "Did you know him?"

"To speak to. Yes, he was a good hand . . . by all I've heard. Killed, wasn't he?"

"Yeah . . . It was Riggin's last case. The one he was working on when he died."

"Too bad. He might have found out who did it."

"Might have? He would have. Maybe he already had, but now we'll never know. We'll never know how much he knew, but we will get Dover's killer."

"You have a lead?"

"A man always leaves tracks, no matter what he does. George Riggin used to say there were no perfect crimes, just imperfect investigations . . . Then, when he kills again—"

"You think he did?"

"Of course." Borden was speaking just loud enough for everyone in the room to hear, if they were listening. And there were enough people in this room to let everybody in town know what he thought. "He killed George Riggin, and then he killed Joe Sackett and Johnny McCoy, and he's tried to kill me."

"If I were you," Hyatt Johnson said, from the next table, "I'd be careful. He's done pretty well so far."

"Maybe . . . but each time he kills he draws the noose tighter. A man leaves a pattern . . . and this man has.

"In fact," he pushed back his chair, "I've got a lead, a good lead. That's why I need Big Injun elsewhere and that's why I'm lettin' Baca out on parole, so I can be free to follow it up. When I get back to town I may know just who did it . . . and why."

"Need help?" Lang asked. "All you've got to do is ask, Bord. I'll lend a hand. Any man in town will."

"I know, but this is a job I have to do myself." He got to his feet. "Come on, Baca, let's get back to the jail. See you tomorrow, Lang. Or the next day. You hold that turkey hunt open. I'll wrap this one up and then we'll do some shooting."

At the jail he showed Baca to his cell, but left the door ajar. "Good a place to sleep as any, and we've both slept in worse. I doubt if I'll see you tomorrow, but keep your eyes open."

"I'll do that." Baca put a hand on the barred door and moved it a few inches. "You really trust a man, don't you?"

"I trust the right man, Baca."

"You think that killer's going after you?" Baca's eyes searched his face. "You think he'll take that risk?"

"He's got to," Borden said quietly. "Look at it. He's running scared. He's killed several times, and now I've told everybody that I've got a lead. The way I see it, he doesn't dare take the risk that I do know something.

"The trouble with crime is, you never know who's watching. You may see nobody, hear nobody. You may be sure nobody is anywhere around, but somebody can be and usually is. There's a bum sleeping in a dark doorway, somebody starting to draw the curtains at an unlighted window, the man who forgets something and comes back up the street. Maybe it's a cowboy who decides to catch himself a bit of sleep under a tree, a woman gathering flowers . . . you never know who's around.

"The way I see it, that killer simply *has* to know. I think he'll follow me to see where I am going and get an idea on what I think I've discovered. And then, when I start back, he'll kill me. Or try."

"You got guts, I'll give you that." Baca sat down on his bunk and pulled off his boots. "I'm going to get myself some shut-eye."

A few minutes later, sitting on the edge of his own bed, Borden Chantry was nowhere nearly so confident. He pulled off his boots, then sat there in the darkness for a moment, staring toward the blank window.

Mora . . . it all came back to Mora. If he just had the time he might ride down there. But he did not have the time. He was facing a showdown he had invited by his words tonight.

He undressed and got into bed. He was wondering again who the killer might be, planning for his ride on the morrow. The trouble was that with all his thinking he forgot the most important item.

He forgot to remember Boone Silva.

For the first time in days he felt free. He had never been a man of the towns, although Bess preferred it to the ranch. Still better, she would have liked to live east, in even larger towns. Yet for him, his life was geared to the open range, out there on the sagebrush levels where the cattle grazed and the long winds blew. He rode slowly, savoring the feel of the wind and the vast sweep of distance around him.

He loved the empty lands, the places where no men were, or few men, at least. Yet he was aware he rode with trouble. Somewhere a man was riding to kill him, and that man might have followed him, might be out there now.

Nor was he deceived by the country, knowing it only too well. Some of the land through which he must ride was rugged, but much seemed rolling or smooth to the eye. But there were many arroyos, many folds in the hills where a horseman might ride unseen, many places where a man might lie in wait.

Suddenly, he changed his route. It was the instinct of the hunted man, for he the hunter was now also the hunted. He put his horse up a steep slope, switched

back along the slope and topped out on a ridge. Yet
with a glance down the far side he crossed over. And
only then, when off the sky-line, did he look about.

Nothing . . . yet? Was that dust? A vague something seemed to hang in the air, but was it dust or
merely the changing colors of the land? The lighter-col-
ored rock or earth of a slope might give the impression
of dust.

He rode back, angling away from his trail toward
the southwest, then veering back toward the northeast.
Several times he paused to listen. When next he neared
the crest of a hill he came to it behind some brush
that he could look through without showing anything
of himself.

Nothing.

He was uneasy. Was it a sixth sense warning him?
A premonition? Or was it simply his knowledge, his
awareness that somebody might be hunting him?

Ed Pearson's place was now only a few miles off,
and a hunter might deduce that was his destination. So
he would circle about and come in from the north. He
cut back sharply, went into the scattered cedar and
circled around. It increased his distance but also his
chances of survival.

Ed's place was in a corner of the hills, a sort of
pocket. He had a rough shack, a corral and a lean-
to shed. Other than an outhouse standing some thirty
yards from the shack, that was all.

The mine tunnel led into the side of the hill not far
back of the shack. There was a dump of whitish earth
spilled down the slope in front of the tunnel, and some
planks to make a runway for his wheelbarrow when
he brought out the waste and the ore.

Whether Ed Pearson had found anything was a
question. Most of the local people chuckled about Ed's
"mine," and agreed among themselves that Ed lived
by killing some rancher's beef now and again, and a
small plot of ground he farmed nearby.

Knowing the quality of man he was, Borden Chantry
approached with care.

A thin trail of smoke lifted from the chimney, and
a couple of horses and a burro stood in the corral.

A horse whinnied as Borden rode down the trail, Winchester in hand, eyes alert.

Here at this time was a moment of danger, for his enemy could easily have guessed where he was riding and gone on before. Yet there was no sound until the last moment when a droop-eared, liver-colored hound came from the door and barked half-heartedly, then came on, whining and wagging its tail.

"Hiya, boy," Borden said to the dog, then lifting his voice he called out. "Ed? This here's Bord Chantry!"

There was no response, no sound.

Warily, Chantry approached the house. He glanced from it to the mine tunnel.

Nothing.

He glanced quickly around at the hills, seeing nothing. He walked his horse up the small slope to the cabin and got down, rifle in hand.

The old hound whined eagerly and started toward the door, then paused, waiting for him.

"Something wrong, boy?" Borden hesitated, uneasy. Slowly, his eyes scanned the area. There was a rusty wheelbarrow turned on its side, and various pieces of rusting iron lay about. The place was a shambles of odds and ends of junk. Pearson was a fixer, and always hauled off everything nobody wanted in the expectation that someday it would come in handy.

The gray, rocky soil sloped away toward a gully that carried off the rain. There was nothing at all in sight, yet he had the feeling of being watched.

He went up to the door, which stood ajar. "Ed?" he put a hand on the door and pushed it wider. It squeaked slightly on rusted hinges.

Inside, the floor was surprisingly clean, swept freshly. On the table stood a coal-oil lamp, still burning but with the wick turned low, a tin plate and a blue enamel cup, a spoon, a fork and a knife. There was a low fire on the hearth, down to coals now, with a slowly steaming coffeepot at the edge of the coals.

A poker lay there, and when he stepped into the door he could see a rumpled and empty bunk of ragged quilts and a moth-eaten buffalo robe.

Items of clothing, old overalls, a pair of worn boots, and some old coats hung from nails in the wall.

A gun belt hung from a peg near the head of the bed where a surprised man might quickly grasp it.

He looked around. A saw and a hammer lay on the floor, a box of candles such as a miner might use, and some odds and ends. There was a bread-box, a barrel that probably contained flour, some few groceries about, and many cans . . . undoubtedly some of the supplies he recently bought.

There was no sign of Ed Pearson.

Chantry walked back to the door and standing well back, looked all around . . . nothing.

Where was Ed Pearson?

He glanced around the shack once more. Everything seemed in place, as if the owner had just stepped out and expected to return at once.

The lean-to shed was open enough, and there was nobody in there . . . yet what about the mine?

That mine had been the source of a good deal of conjecture. It was widely doubted that any ore existed there, yet Ed succeeded in making a living, and was reported to occasionally have gold dust to sell, or nuggets.

Chantry walked to the cupboard and took down another blue enameled cup, with a little of the enamel chipped from the rim. He glanced at it, distrusting the cleanliness of such cantankerous old bachelors as Pearson, but the cup was spotless. He took up the pot and poured himself a cup.

It was black as sin and strong enough to curl a man's hair, but it was hot, and it tasted good. Cup in hand, he walked almost to the door . . . but not quite.

A lizard darted halfway across the doorstep, then stopped, panting.

A rider was coming down the far slope.

Chapter XV

It was not Ed Pearson.

It was a long-geared man on a lean strawberry roan that looked to be built for speed as well as staying power, a mighty good horse for any cowhand to be riding. Suddenly, without knowing why he did it, Borden Chantry unpinned his badge and thrust it into his vest pocket.

The man had a lean, sallow face with greasy black hair hanging to his shoulders. He wore a fancy black jacket sewn with beads and spotted with grease stains. He looked at Chantry for a long minute.

"Howdy," he said.

" 'Light an' set," Chantry suggested.

"Passin' by," the man still studied him with blue-gray, flat-looking eyes that revealed nothing. "How far's town?"

"Hour . . . maybe more."

The snake eyes did not waver. "Your place?"

"Stopping by," Chantry was waiting, as was the other man. Each was silent, probing, listening for some indication that would tell him about the other man.

The stranger jerked his head to indicate the tunnel. "What's he got?"

Chantry shrugged. "Says it's gold. Nobody ever found any gold here, and I never saw any of his."

"Beats all . . . stayin' in a place like this." The man looked around, his head turning slowly, without any movement from his body, then the eyes came back to Chantry.

"Who's the law over yonder?"

"Name of Chantry . . . used to be a rancher until a freeze-up killed his stock."

"Good with a gun?"

"He gets along."

The stranger turned his horse, then looked back. Chantry shifted his position a little to keep his right hand free, and when the stranger looked back his eyes riveted on Chantry's side above the belt. Instantly, Borden knew that the movement of his body had pushed part of the badge up from his vest pocket. Chantry did not make the mistake of looking down.

The man looked at Chantry, his black eyes no longer flat and dull. "You Chantry?"

"I am. Are you Boone Silva?"

The eyes flickered, ever so slightly. "Uh-huh." Then a hand gestured toward the badge. "Quittin'? Why you got it off?"

"No, not quitin'. It doesn't count for much out here. I'm the town marshal."

"See you in town?"

"I'll be around."

Silva raised a negligent hand, and cantered away. Borden Chantry watched him go, then took up the rifle from beside the door.

With his left hand he lifted the cup. The coffee was cold. He threw it out, took the cup to the sink and spilled water from a bucket to rinse it out, then walked back to the door. Dust lingered in the air. All was still, the sun was very hot. His Appaloosa stood, head dropping, standing three-legged in the sunshine.

The dog whined and he put a hand on his head. "What's the matter, old fellow? Where's Ed?"

He went to the spring with an old bucket and dipped up water for his horse. While the Appaloosa drank, he looked around. He'd better have a look at the mine tunnel . . . It had been more than a year since he'd been out this way, but Ed worked on it by fits and starts, and Ed might be up there.

When the horse had drunk its fill, he refilled the bucket for the dog, poured a little in the dog's dish and put the rest of it in the shade. Then, rifle in hand, he walked up the slight slope to the opening.

There were tools about, and an empty can that had held black powder. He saw the circles on the earth where at least two other cans had stood. He stepped into the mouth of the tunnel and called out, "Ed?"

No sound, no response. He took a step further and called out again. "Ed? Are you there? This is Chantry."

Nothing . . . Suddenly, just beyond the reach of his eyes, in the darkness where little light fell . . . Was that a boot?

He started forward, his ankle hooked on a wire or string and he fell forward knowing even as he fell what had happened. The blast of the explosion knocked him flat on the floor of the tunnel. The tremendous blast, augmented by the close confines of the tunnel, seemed to split the mountain apart, and then there was a rending of mine timbers, a crashing of rocks, a trickle of gravel and sand. Then silence and the dust.

He lay perfectly still, perfectly conscious. His every sense was alert, yet he did not move, letting the dust settle slowly, the last trickle of gravel come to an end.

A trap had been set and he had blundered into it. And now he was entombed . . . buried alive.

Unless he could do something, he was dead.

He pushed himself up to his knees. There were broken rocks all about him, and some splintered timbers. Rocks and dirt fell away from his legs as he got up. He stooped, felt around, and found his rifle.

The mine was completely black, for closed off as it was there was a total absence of light. With no light at all, he would see no better no matter how long he remained here.

He needed light desperately, and felt in his pocket for matches. Ed Pearson would have some candles, somewhere . . . But where?

Would he bring a fresh one to the mine each time? Or would he . . . it seemed more logical . . . keep a store of them in the tunnel itself?

But where? And how deep was the tunnel?

He found matches, and taking one out, struck it, shielding it carefully with his hand against any puff of wind caused by a further fall.

In the dim light of its glow, he looked around.

He saw only the rocks, the dark tunnel ahead . . . and on the floor of the tunnel the body of Ed Pearson. He had been shot through the head.

Suddenly, on a shelf of rock, Chantry saw a faint sheen of white . . . The candles!

He took down one of the candles and lighted it, then looked around. There was no comfort in what his eyes told him.

The pile of broken rock and timber had fallen back toward him. And judging by the distance he had advanced into the opening, and the position of Pearson's body, he was at least fifty feet into the opening now. And fifty feet or more of deep rock lay between him and the entrance.

Digging out would not be impossible—if there was no further caving. But what if he spent all that time, and used what air remained, only to have a sudden slide cover the mine entrance? True, the slide might not be great, coming off that hill, yet it could be many tons. And the roof of the tunnel looked none too secure as it was.

Was there another opening? From time to time Chantry seemed to feel a faint movement of air, although that might be his imagination, for the candle flame stood straight and still.

Would not Pearson have made another entrance? An opening for ventilation? Or for escape if need be?

There was a shovel there, and a pick, several drills and a double jack. He recalled seeing a single jack just outside the mine entrance, where Pearson must have been using it for a hammer.

Rifle in one hand, candle in the other, Borden Chantry went off down the tunnel. There were several crosscuts, none of them very deep, but he saw few signs that indicated ore.

Pearson had been a man who lived much to himself, and had never welcomed visitors. And western people being what they were, they left him to his own devices. For every man was free to choose his own life-style as long as he did not encroach.

Borden Chantry had no illusions. He was trapped. Buried alive. Nobody was going to find him and dig him out in the time he had left, and whatever was done, he must do. And quickly. He turned his mind sharply away from thoughts of death, and tried to see clearly just what his position was and what he had to work with.

He doubted that the murderer had known Pearson any better than he did, if as well. Therefore, the murderer could not have known the layout of this tunnel, or mine, or whatever it was. He could only have known the usual gossip that was talked.

Furthermore, there was small chance that the man had the time to explore. Once he had guessed the direction in which Chantry was riding, he must have come straight here, killed Pearson, and set his trap. The ruthlessness of the man, and his willingness to kill, was appalling.

Or was it Boone Silva who had done this? In either case the result was the same . . . Yet from what he knew of Silva this was not his style.

Chantry stopped short. Suddenly the tunnel had ended.

He stood in a somewhat circular area where Pearson had stoped out a space. On three sides there was broken rock in huge chunks, a few leaning slabs, and much debris. Holding his candle high, Chantry could see the stope was a death trap, for great slabs still hung, half broken free, ready for a shock to drop them. Even where such slabs did not exist, there was plenty of stuff that needed barring down before a man could work there.

Turning, he walked back up the drift. Putting his candle on a small ledge in the wall, he put down his rifle, took off his coat, and went to work.

The air was not too bad yet. How long he could hope to survive he could not guess, but Chantry was not a man to give up. He worked with his hands at first, rolling back huge chunks of rock or tilting slabs out of the way. When he could he started with the shovel, but it was slow work.

He glanced at his watch, then worked on. At the end of an hour, he tried to gauge his progress, and it was so small that it sent a shiver of dread through him.

Of course, he would not need a large hole, and even

a small one would permit fresh air to come in. Again he went to work, crawling up toward the place where the pile of debris met the roof.

No longer did he permit himself to think of or judge the time. He simply worked. Time consumed meant nothing to him now, for he was working against death.

Rock after rock he pulled back and rolled away. He could not use a shovel on much of it, although a pick was of use at times. He stopped finally, mopping the salty sweat from around his eyes and trying to catch his breath.

The space where he sat was close and hot. He crawled down off the muck pile and sat on a slab of rock, mopping his face. If only his Appaloosa would go home! Lang Adams or Kim Baca might track him back to the Pearson place and see what had happened. Then he'd have a chance . . . a small chance, but a chance.

The Appaloosa was used to standing, ground-hitched. It might be some time before he moved off, and Pearson was unlikely to have visitors.

After a few minutes Chantry got up and went back to work. He had no gloves and his hands had soon been brutally torn and scraped, but he tried not to worry or hurry, just to work steadily and methodically. He knew that therein lay his only chance . . . a slim one at that.

Soon he had burrowed out a hole twice his own length. Maybe he had moved twelve feet of earth . . . Nearly forty feet to go, if his estimate was right.

Forty feet! It was too much. He worked on and on. Twice the earth caved in and he had the job to go over, but he continued at the same pace, closing his mind to all but what he had to do.

After awhile he crawled out again. And when he was close to the candle, he peered at his watch.

Four hours . . . and he had done so little. He lighted a second candle from the stub of the first. The flame was eating up air but mentally, he needed it. The darkness was like a tomb, and the flickering candlelight was some measure of hope.

He returned to work. In a few more minutes, he

was totally halted. A huge slab, its dimensions unknown, had fallen like a door across his tunnel, blocking all advance. It had fallen flat-side toward him, and there it was, a giant barrier. Working toward the right side of the slab, which was where the open tunnel should be had it not been full of muck, Chantry uncovered three feet of the slab before he came to an edge. Behind it a heavy chunk of rock that must weigh all of two hundred pounds had fallen and was wedged tightly.

Slowly, he backed out of his hole. He mopped the sweat from his face.

His mouth and throat were dry, and he had no water. He sat down on the slab again and rested, trying to think clearly. He felt dull and heavy. Perhaps the air was almost used up. He glanced at the candle . . . a still, clear flame. But a while ago he had remembered it as flickering . . . That was a trick the mind could play, for folks usually spoke of a flickering candle. He got up and crawled back in his hole to stare at the boulder, and then to begin digging with the pick, working smaller rocks from under it.

He worked and worked, and after a long time the boulder sagged forward into the hollow he had dug out. There was a clear space above it now—but not enough. Not over six inches . . . and no air was coming through.

Returning for the candle, he crawled back and held the candle high to see better. There was a sort of hollow behind the boulder and the slab, a good two feet of empty space where he would not have to dig . . . *if* he could get that boulder out.

He worked at its base until his shoulders ached, and at last it gave and dropped a few inches further. Now he could at least reach beyond it. He did not then begin, though. He backed out of his hole, taking the candle with him, and sat down on the slab.

He was tired, desperately tired. He lighted another candle and looked at his watch . . . nine hours.

He had been imprisoned here for nine hours. It must be the middle of the night. His lids felt heavy and he wanted to rest . . . Well, just a few minutes.

Stretching out on the floor of the tunnel he cradled his head on his hat and was almost instantly asleep.

Something cold and wet touched his cheek, and he fought himself out of a heavy sleep, struggling up. Reaching out, his hand struck something hairy and wet. He gasped, jerking back his hand. And then, in the feeble light of the burned-down candle, he saw a glistening, cringing shape. It whined and dropped to the floor, head on its paws.

Pearson's dog!

But how . . . ? He got up so quickly he staggered, and the dog sprang back in dismay, but when he put out a hand to it the dog came eagerly forward. "It's all right, fellow," he said gently. "But how the devil did you get here?"

He took up his rifle and the candle, and the dog, knowing that he meant to go, started back down the tunnel, running. Fearing he would lose it, he ran also. The dog reached the round stope at the end of the tunnel, and turned swiftly up among the rocks and disappeared behind a slab.

Chantry felt the excitement go out of him. The dog had probably found some wet hole that only it could get through, but if the dog could get in, then air could also. He clambered up the rocks and looked behind the slab, which had seemed to lie almost flat against the wall.

It did nothing of the kind. There was an opening there, dark and dripping, but an opening.

He lowered himself down and peered into the four-foot hole. Water dripped from some hidden spring in the rocks, but not twenty feet away he could see the gray of the outer night.

The dog had run on ahead, and now stood waiting for him, and he crawled after. It was dirty, muddy, and wet, but he got through, crawled outside and stood up.

He was alive and free.

It was night . . . almost morning by the look of the stars . . . and he just stood still and breathed in the cool night air. Nothing in all his life had ever tasted better.

Turning, he knelt, bathed off his bloody hands, and shook the water from them. Then taking up his rifle, he walked around the hill, following the dog, to Pearson's shack.

All was dark and still. Yet as he approached the house, something moved and his horse whinnied softly.

Taking up the reins, he led the horse to the cabin door, which he pushed shut. Then he stepped into the saddle.

"Come on, boy," he said to the dog. "You'd better come with me."

It would be good to get home.

Chapter XVI

When Borden Chantry awakened in the cool dawn, he had slept no more than three hours, but what awakened him he did not know. Yet he awoke with an awareness of danger.

He swung his feet to the floor and dressed quietly, not to awaken Bess. Then he went to the kitchen. To his surprise, Billy McCoy was there, and he already had coffee on.

"Used to make it for Pa," he said. He looked down at Chantry's hands, which were swollen and raw. "Boy! What did you do to yourself?"

Chantry explained quietly and the boy stared at him, awed. "It was the same man who killed your pa, Billy. Now he's killed Ed Pearson. I guess I'm not much of a marshal, to let him run loose so long."

"I'm huntin' him, too," Billy said, quietly.

"You?" Chantry was startled. "You leave that to me, Billy."

"He killed my pa."

"I know, and I know how you feel. But leave it to me. That sort of feeling was all right in the days when there was no law. But there is law now, and we've got to let the law do its work."

He paused. "I'm closer than I think, Billy, that's why he's scared. He's trying hard to kill me before I catch up with him. I expected him to follow me out of town and try to kill me, but I thought he'd try to dry-gulch me." Borden paused, watching Billy pour coffee. "He might use that same old fifty-two he's used a few times."

"No, he won't," Billy said grimly. "He won't use no fifty-two no more. Because I got it."

"What?"

Billy flushed. "Marshal, I maybe shouldn't ha' done

it, but I swiped his rifle. That night in the barn? He'd hidden his rifle in that ol' barrel, an' I got it before he could get back. That was me in the barn that night when he slugged you. He never seen me, on'y we nearly run together in the barn. But I got that rifle and got out."

Borden Chantry had felt like swearing only a few times in his life. But this was one of the times when he wanted to do a really first-rate job of cussing.

"Damn it, Billy, you're concealing evidence! You could go to jail for that!"

"I know it," Billy said glumly. "I was sore. I wanted I should shoot him with his own gun, so I cached it."

"Billy, that rifle may be an important clue. I must have it. But above all, I don't want anyone, and I mean *anyone,* to know you had it or that you were in the barn that night. Do you understand?"

"You think he'd try to kill me, Marshal?"

"He most certainly would, Billy, and we've had enough killing. Now where is the rifle?"

."Right there in the barn. I never taken it out. It's a-layin' atop one o' them rafters, the third one from the door. I got up on the manger and laid her right there so's he wouldn't catch me with it."

"Billy . . . who is he?"

"Durned if I know! I never did git to see him! It was all dark in there, an' then I heard something stirrin' an' I was just a-waitin' for a chancet to run. When it come, I taken out."

"Billy, I want you to think. I want you to try to remember. There just might be something . . . Billy, did you know Pin Dover?"

"Sure! He punched cows with Pa. When he come to town, they used to talk over the old times. Pin was down to Mora when the land grant fights were on, an' Pa knowed a lot of the folks who were in on that fight."

"Did they ever mention anybody here in town who had been in Mora?"

"No . . . nobody I can recall. I did hear Pa say one time that Hyatt Johnson had been down there. He was some sort of friend to the man who brought in all those folks to squat on the land."

Chantry finished his coffee and got to his feet. "I'll eat breakfast at the Bon-Ton. You can tell Bess when she gets up. I've got to see a man."

"You going to get that rifle?"

"You ain't just a-whoofin'. I'm going to get it right off."

He started walking. The town was waking up. A couple of men were on the boardwalk, sweeping it off. Hurley was sweeping in front of the Corral Saloon, and Ed was in front of the Bon-Ton.

"Can you fix me some eggs?" Chantry let his eyes run along the street toward the bank. It was early. Hyatt would not be in yet. Which meant he would be at home where he could see anybody at the freighter's barn . . . but so could others.

"Make those eggs over about medium, Ed," he said, "with a slab of ham . . . a thick slab. I'm going over to the barn for a minute."

He crossed the street and walked along south of the Corral Saloon, then went to the barn.

All was dark and still. Light fell through a few cracks and there was still a smell of hay and of leather hanging about the place.

The third rafter . . . it was a likely place. He got up on the edge of a stall and reached it easily. He had just stepped down when somebody spoke.

"What have you got there?"

It was Lang Adams.

"Howdy, Lang! Had breakfast? I just ordered me some ham and. Come on over and I'll stand treat."

Adams shook his head doubtfully. "Bord, you're the hardest man to find . . . I was hunting you yesterday, and nobody had any idea where you were. Why, I went all over town!"

"I rode out to Ed Pearson's place." He was carrying the rifle in his left hand, muzzle down. "Somebody shot him."

"Him, too? I don't like it, Bord. I'm in the notion of going up to Denver until this is all over, or to Fort

Worth or somewhere. This man doesn't care who he kills."

"You sure it's a man?"

"Why, sure. Why I never thought . . . What gave you the idea it might not be?"

Chantry shrugged. "We can't rule anybody out, and a woman can pull a trigger as well as a man."

They walked to the Bon-Ton and took seats.

Breakfast came and they carried on a casual conversation of horses, cattle, range conditions and new arrivals.

"Boone Silva's in town," Chantry commented. "Huntin' me."

"Boone Silva? Who is he?"

"Nobody much. He's packed a gun in a couple of range wars and done some shooting for hire here and there, but somebody sent for him. Somebody from town. So far as I know the man most wanted dead right now is me. Anyway, Boone and me had a talk about it."

"A *talk?*" Lang was shocked.

"You mean the man's hunting you, and you actually talked to him? Where was this?"

"Out at Pearson's. I reckon I'll have him to handle one of these days. Maybe sooner than late."

"But he's a gunfighter, Bord. I never heard that you were—"

"Oh, I guess I can handle myself. Anyway, I never did set up to be a gunfighter . . . I don't think anybody does, really. It just sort of happens that way, and when a man wins a few fights he gets a reputation whether he wants it or not. I always shied away from anything of the kind."

"You be careful."

"He won't give me any trouble. In fact, I think I'll just throw him in jail until this is all over."

Lang Adams swore. "Bord, you beat all. You mean you'd try to *arrest* him? Boone Silva? He'd kill you."

The idea had come to Chantry as he talked, and instantly, the practicality of it struck him. He had his hands full trying to find a murderer without worrying about a gun battle with Silva. And he had nothing but impatience for such men, anyway. Fortunately, there were few of them, and jail was the place.

He got up suddenly. "Lang, you finish your coffee. I've got a job to do."

He walked out on the street. Silva would likely be at the hotel.

Borden Chantry walked to the hotel and switched the register around. Boone Silva was in Room 12.

Elsie came up, touching her hair with quick fingers. "Anything I can do for you, Marshal?"

"Has Silva gone out?"

"No . . . no, he hasn't." She looked at him quickly. "Borden, there isn't going to be any trouble, is there? I just finished patching up the bullet holes from the last fight. Now I don't want—"

"Relax, Elsie. I just want to talk to the man."

He went down the hall and tapped on the door. "Water an' towels!" he said. "Water an' towels!"

"Don't need any!" Silva's voice was irritable. "Let a man sleep!"

"Boone? This is Chantry. I want to talk to you."

Borden had his six-shooter in his hand, and when the door opened, so did Silva. They faced each other with scarcely three feet between them, both holding .44-calibre weapons.

"I'm arresting you, Silva," Borden said mildly. "Taking you down to jail where you can stay out of trouble."

"I'm not in trouble."

"Preventive medicine, Silva. Let's just say we have a quiet town here, with no business for paid gunmen, and we want to keep it that way. Now give me your gun and come along."

"Like *hell*!"

Borden Chantry smiled. Such men as Boone Silva liked to kill, but they trusted in their speed and marksmanship—and in the present case there was a chance for neither. Whatever skill Boone might have was negated by the reason of position. At the distance neither man could miss, and at the distance both would probably die. And Borden Chantry was banking that Silva did not want to die.

His was a slight advantage due to the fact that he knew a good deal about Silva, and Silva didn't know much about him. Silva did not know how crazy he might be, and the very fact that Chantry had approached him in this manner indicated that Chantry didn't care . . . Although as a matter of fact he did care, and very much.

"You'll die, too," Silva said.

"Sure . . . but it's my job. You can make a buck anywhere, Silva. This is only one more town to you, only one more job."

"You scared to meet me out in the street?"

"I'm meeting you right here, Silva. Now hand me that gun—or die."

For just a moment, Silva stared at him. Then slowly, very carefully, he reversed his gun.

"Take your finger out of the trigger guard, Silva. Hand it to me by the barrel only."

Chantry took the gun and Silva said, "Now let me get my pants on."

"No, Silva. Just as you are, in your drawers."

"Damn you, I'll—!"

"After you get out, Silva. Not now. Come on."

Prissy was sweeping the boardwalk in front of the post office. And George Blazer had come to the door of the stage office to carry on a conversation with Hyatt Johnson, who was crossing from the store to the bank. All conversation stopped when Boone Silva walked up the street in his long underwear, barefooted and furious. Borden Chantry walked two feet behind him, his pistol in its holster, Boone's gun in his waistband.

Lang Adams came to the door of the Bon-Ton, coffeecup in hand, Ed beside him. Lang stared, then he swore softly.

"Ever see the like?" Ed commented, pleased. "We got us a marshal, Lang. That Boone Silva will never live this down . . . never!"

"There's only one thing he can do now," Lang said. "He's got to kill Chantry."

It was Big Injun who opened the door for them, but Kim Baca was seated on the settee at one side of the room. He looked up, grinning. "Howdy, Boone! Welcome to the ol' homestead!"

"Go to hell!" Boone said irritably.

He walked into the cell and the door clanged shut behind him. The key turned in the lock.

"You'll never get away with this, Marshal. What charge are you holding me on?"

Chantry smiled. "I'll think of something, Boone. Disturbing the peace, maybe, or loitering. Or indecent exposure. You see, Boone, I'm doing this for your own good. There have been several murders committed around here, and we don't know who did them. Folks are getting mighty upset about it, and they want to see somebody in jail for them, or hung for them.

"I can prove you were at Pearson's and Pearson was killed, so you're the only tangible thing they have to put a hand on.

"We can't prove you killed those other folks, but you can't prove you didn't. You might be able, given time, to prove you were somewhere else when some of them were killed, but that would take time, and you mightn't have that time.

"So," Chantry kept his face straight, "I just had to save you, Boone. I had to keep your neck from being stretched, and the only way I could do it was throw you in jail. Even if that's not strictly true, it gives you something to feel good about.

"The grub's not bad here. There's magazines and newspapers around, and you look tired, Boone. I think you need a rest. So just lie back there on your bunk and relax. Later, when I have time, I'll bring your clothes to you. For now you'll do just fine."

He walked into the outer office, closing the door behind him. Baca looked up, quizzically. "You haven't headed him off, Marshal, just postponed it. Now, when he gets out, he'll have to kill you."

"One thing at a time, Baca. One thing at a time."

Chapter XVII

"You asked that I should keep an eye on things," Baca said then. "It was almighty quiet around, Marshal. Your wife took the buckboard out . . . drove into the country, but she wasn't gone long."

Bess? Where would *she* be going?

"Anybody else?"

"Well, I didn't see the banker around. I dropped in on Blazer . . . he was there. And that youngster who's living at your place . . . the McCoy kid? He was all over town. I never did see such a busy kid."

Of course, one man could not watch everywhere. And the murderer must have been alert, curious as to why Kim Baca had been released, and therefore wary. And there was always the arroyo behind the town. It was all too easy to slip into that arroyo and simply vanish.

Seated at the battered desk in the office, Chantry tipped back in his chair and closed his eyes. Yet he was not asleep, and did not plan to sleep. Slowly, methodically, he went over the impressions he had, and the little, so very little evidence.

He now had the .52-calibre the murderer had used on some occasions, but he had no record of such a gun. And no one to whom he talked remembered having seen it.

He got up suddenly. "Hold the fort," he said, "I'll be at the Bon-Ton."

He went out on the street and stood there, looking up and down, thinking. A vague impression was stirring around in his mind. He knew several people who had some connection with Mora, but how many might have a connection of which he knew nothing?

Revenge was always a possibility as a motive for murder. But the revenge killer usually committed his act where the victim would know who was killing him, and why. Not always, of course.

Chantry considered himself no kind of a thinker, yet it seemed to him that it all came back to some reason that lay outside of the town itself. Somebody, somewhere, wanted to keep something covered up.

Because he or she feared arrest? Or because he or she stood to gain by keeping something under cover?

Most of the dealings—financial and otherwise—were known to everybody in a small town. Not much could be concealed. So who in the town stood to gain anything? Enough of anything to make murder acceptable?

Pin Dover had returned from Mora and shortly after had been killed.

George Riggin had been on the verge of uncovering the killer, and he had been killed . . . by accident or otherwise.

Joe Sackett had ridden into town from Mora, and he had been killed.

Johnny McCoy had seen or known something, and he had been killed. Johnny had also been to Mora and was acquainted with Dover.

Now Ed Pearson had been killed . . . because he knew something? Might know something? Or just to get him out of the way so that Borden Chantry might be killed?

There had to be a design, a pattern, somewhere. When you trailed a man or an animal, you had to figure out where that man or animal might be going. And if you could, that was a help.

So where was the murderer going?

Why did people kill? Hate, revenge, jealousy, and for money . . . those were the obvious reasons.

But who hated Pin Dover? Nobody. Who wanted anything he had? Nobody. A kill for revenge? Dover had been around for years, and if the killer was a local man, why had he waited?

Joe Sackett had been a stranger, so nobody had reason to hate him.

The only fact was Mora . . . and again Chantry came to the conclusion that all of them had been killed for something they knew—or that the killer suspected they knew.

It must be a question of money.

Putting the thought aside, he returned to Pin Dover. His had been the first killing, and on his return from Mora.

The thought came to him suddenly and he shook it off. Ridiculous!

He walked slowly along the street to the Bon-Ton.

Boone Silva lay on his back in his cell in his underwear. His fury was wearing off, and good sense was taking over. He had the cunning of a wild animal, knowing what was good for him and what was bad. He lived dangerously, but with an inner wariness that kept him ever on the alert.

Now he admitted, with grudging admiration, that Chantry had taken him fairly. He went over it again in his mind . . . Should he have gambled and fired?

No. Had he done so he now would be dead . . . By this time, buried. And he was very much alive. Would Borden Chantry have fired? He asked himself that question and remembered Chantry's eyes . . . Yes, Chantry would have fired. It took nerve to face a man like that, at point-blank range.

Now at a distance . . . That would be a different story. Boone Silva had killed a number of men, but he was faster than most, and a much better shot, so his chances were good—far better than average. When he drew a gun on a man, that man was dead.

Sometimes he had tried to imagine a man faster than himself. Silva could not make himself believe such a man existed . . . or that if he was faster, he could shoot straighter.

Someday, out on the street, he would meet Borden Chantry.

His mind reverted to the job that brought him to town. He had come to kill Chantry. He would get five hundred dollars when it was done.

The arrangements had been made in the usual way. There was a hole in the rock out at Mesa de Maya that was his post office, a place where a select few people knew he could be reached. He had gone to that hole in the rock one day and found a name and a town and a note that meant five hundred dollars when Chantry was dead.

It was all very simple. When he had done his job, he would ride to a certain saloon and would pick up an envelope.

Five hundred dollars was a lot of money. At thirty dollars a month, the going wage for a cowhand, it was almost two years' work.

He thought of Borden Chantry again. They had said he was a rancher, temporarily marshal. That might very well be true, but Borden Chantry was no bargain. Boone Silva wanted, for his pride's sake, to face him in the open and shoot him down. But his animal caution told him that would be foolish—very foolish, indeed. When they let him out of jail he would say, "No hard feelin's, Marshal," and ride out of town. Then he'd circle around, have a fast horse ready and another one five miles away. And then, with one shot from his rifle, he'd cut Chantry down . . . and be out of the Territory before they knew what had happened.

Five hundred dollars was a lot of money only if you lived to spend it.

A faint curiosity stirred him. Who was it that wanted Chantry dead?

Usually it was some cow rustler they couldn't pin anything on, or a nester who squatted on some rancher's best water. Silva had an idea this was something different.

He had looked over the town on his way in, sizing up his chances, his easiest escape route, the best available places from which to shoot.

Kim Baca strolled back and straddled a chair, facing the bars. "You treed yourself an ol' he-coon," he commented.

"Yeah? He ain't so much."

"Caught me," Baca added.

Silva rolled up on one elbow. "Then what you doin' out there?"

Baca explained. "Hell, why not? It's better out here than in there, an' he's a square-shooter, Chantry is. Might see me on my way when this is over."

" 'This'?"

"Been a string of murders," Kim commented, "one after the other. And somebody's worried the marshal is gettin' close. That's why they called you in . . . to kill him before he can lay it on them."

"Who?"

"Figured maybe you knew."

"I don't know nothin'. Wouldn't tell you if I did."

"This here marshal. I don't know him much better than you, but he stacks up like a square-shooter. You know as well as I do that he's got a chance to clean off the record by just sticking you with all these killings, but he ain't going to do it. He'll keep you here to keep you out of his hair, and then he'll turn you loose."

"And then I'll kill him."

"Be a damn fool if you tried. You an' me know there's many a man around, ranchers, freighters, cowhands and whatever, that are just as good with a gun as some of the marshals and gunfighters. Only they don't have the name, and they don't want it.

"Take me, f'r instance. I expect I'm as fast with a gun as you, but I just steal horses. Not *any* horse . . . I steal only the best, like that gelding of yours."

"You lay off that horse, Baca. You lay off, or—"

"Or? You don't scare me a mite, Boone, not a mite. You didn't scare Borden Chantry, either. I'm not going to steal your horse because you're going to need him to get out of town on before folks around here have themselves a necktie party with you wearin' the tie. There's been talk, you know." Kim Baca was lying cheerfully. There had been no talk. The townspeople trusted in their marshal, and so did he, but it was one way to build a fire under Silva. And there was precedent. More than one western town had become impatient with lawlessness and proceeded to string up several who happened to be handy. And a couple of times they had picked up relatively harmless men who happened to enjoy the company of outlaws. Like that fellow Russian Bill, down in Shakespeare, New Mexico.

Boone Silva tried not to look worried, but he looked around suddenly, like a trapped animal. "I got to get out of here."

"Don't try it, Boone. As long as you're in here,

you're safe. You get out there where the marshal can't protect you, an' you wouldn't have a chance. You set right where you're at, but take it from me. When he turns you loose . . . leave. Don't get any fancy notions."

For a half hour then, Baca rambled along on other things, horses, killings, ways of making contact. And after a bit Boone Silva loosened up a little. He did not tell Baca where or how, only that there was a way he could be reached to do a job.

"How many men know how to reach you? I'd be scared one of them would be loose-tongued."

"Not a chance! Only four men know how to reach me with a deal. And anybody wants me has to go to one of the four, and he passes the word along."

After awhile, Kim Baca left Silva and walked back into the office. He sat down and put his feet on the desk. It was almost as if he was a deputy . . . Well, that wouldn't be a bad job, come to think of it.

He was tilted back in his chair when Lang Adams stuck his head in the door. "Bord around?"

"Down to the Bon-Ton. He thinks better with a cup of coffee."

"I hear he's got Boone Silva in jail?"

"He has . . . I'm just keeping him out of trouble, Mr. Adams, and out of Chantry's hair while he solves this murder binge."

"He'll solve it, too," Lang commented. "Once he gets his teeth into it, he doesn't let go."

"You're right. Was I the killer, I'd pull my stakes. No matter what he wants out of this town, it won't do him any good in prison or hanging at the end of a rope.

"You know something, Mr. Adams? Folks around here don't know what they've got. That Borden Chantry is the smoothest operator I've seen, and I've seen a few.

"He took me slick as a whistle. No shooting, no sweat. It was cold-turkey. And he did the same with Boone Silva. Nine men out of ten would have turned both of those affairs into shootin' matches, but he didn't. I tell you, he's just a whole lot smarter than folks give him credit for."

"I think you're right, Baca." Lang Adams leaned on

the doorjamb. "I've heard you're pretty good with a gun yourself."

"I don't advertise it. When I have to use a gun, I use it. But I'll never draw on any man if I can avoid it. A dead man makes a bad pillow for comfortable sleeping."

Lang Adams went back to the street. It was only a few steps to the Bon-Ton, yet he stopped in the post office and asked for mail. There was only his St. Louis newspaper, but no note from Blossom . . . He should ride out there.

He glanced at himself in the post office window as he left. He looked thinner . . . Was he scared? A lot of people in town were, and many of them were not coming out on the streets at night. Lang Adams knew how they felt.

Borden Chantry was alone at his table near the window. He looked up as Adams stepped in. "Howdy, Lang. Pull up a chair."

"Stopped by the office. Baca said you were down here." Lang glanced at him. "You really trust him, don't you?"

"I do. He gave me his word, Lang, and I've known many a horse thief who wouldn't break his word. Maybe elsewhere, but not in this country. And Kim Baca prides himself on it."

"Folks are getting edgy, Bord."

"They should be. There's been more killings than in the last Indian outbreak, and nobody in jail yet. But I'll get the guilty one."

"You think it might be a woman? You mentioned that?"

"Could be. I can't think of more than one or two women in town who could have run with George Riggin's saddle. And the killer did."

"I meant to ask you about that. Why would George leave his saddle to you? You of all people? You've got some saddles."

"Oh, sentiment, I guess! George was always like a second father to me."

"He was a good man. Too bad he had to die that way, but accidents happen to all of us."

"It was no accident, Lang. I went back there and checked out the spot where that boulder fell on him, and I found where somebody used a lever to pry it loose. At that, it only knocked him from his horse and stunned him. Then the killer walked over him and dropped a rock on his head."

"I'll be damned! How could you figure that out?"

"I talked to Doc after I looked the ground over. And I found where his body had fallen, and Doc told me he'd been hit twice by that rock. The second time, the rock was dropped on him, on the side of his head as he lay on the ground. There's no way a falling rock could have killed him."

"Baca was right. He said you were better than we knew."

Chantry shook his head. "No, Lang, I'm not. But a killer like this is his own worst enemy. Each time he kills he draws the noose tighter, just as he thinks he's killing people that might pin it on him. After awhile he simply offers himself up on a platter."

Lang Adams shook his head. "I don't agree with you. The trouble is that nobody ever hears of the men who kill or steal and get away with it. You only hear of the ones who get caught."

"Had a puncher who worked for me one time, Lang. Folks said he was the slickest horse and cow thief around, and he'd robbed banks, too. Some eastern feller came out here and wrote a song about him. You know, Lang, that man worked for me because he was hungry and needed a place to eat and sleep. And he worked hard, too. He was right proud of that song, and of all the talk about him. But one time we got to talking and from one thing and another it developed that here he was closing in on sixty years old, and he'd no place to go and nobody much who wanted him."

"Could happen, I suppose."

"It did happen. But that wasn't the worst of it, Lang. This slick crook they were singing that ballad about, he was sixty years old, and he'd spent forty years of that time in prison."

Chapter XVIII

After Lang Adams went back to the store, Borden Chantry reached into his pocket and took out the tally book George Riggin had left hidden in the secret pocket of his saddle.

It was a thin little book with not much written in it, but enough.

He studied it for a long time before he closed the book and slipped it back into his pocket. He refilled his cup as Ed came out.

"Coffee all right, Marshal?" Ed sat down opposite him. "Pie's good, and it's on the house."

"Thanks. I'll stick to the coffee."

"That Baca was in . . . Seems like a nice boy."

"He's all right. He just likes better horses than he can afford." He tasted the coffee. "Ed, has Hyatt Johnson been in?"

"Not yet. Nobody's been in but Blossom Galey. She was looking kind of down in the mouth, I figured. Not right for a woman who's about to get married."

"You mean to Lang?"

"They ain't keepin' it a secret, Marshal. Blossom's a good woman, and she surely has built that ranch into something. Does a sight better than when her old man had it. He was a good cattleman but had no head for business. Blossom, she's got both. That gal's no fool, no fool at all. Why, when she gets Ed Pearson's place—"

"Ed Pearson's place? How would she get that?"

"Figured you knew, Marshal. I think most folks do. Blossom grub-staked Ed two, three times. And the last time, she taken a mortgage on his place. And the way it figures, if anything happened to him, she would take possession.

"He's got good water out there, you know. And that sort of fills in that corner for her. Once she marries Lang, she'll have . . . or they will have . . . his place. I

tell you, Marshal, that Blossom will be the richest
woman in this corner of the state!"

What a damned fool he'd been! Blossom Galey was
not only a pretty woman, but a smart one. And tough,
too. She'd caught a rustler at one of her calves once,
and she winged him when he went for a gun, then
brought him in herself. She was a good shot, a dead
shot.

And her pa had been a buffalo hunter. Just the kind
of a man who might own a .52-calibre rifle of the old
style.

He got up suddenly. Maybe . . . just maybe . . . he
had it figured out.

There were still a couple of things he had to know.
Just a couple.

He walked over to the jail. Big Injun was sitting in
the chair outside. "You saw those tracks? The tracks
left by the man who killed Sackett's horse?"

Big Injun just looked at him.

"Big Injun, you know the track of every horse in the
country. You can read sign like I read a sign on a store-
front. Whose horse was that?"

"Your horse. Big gray horse, not Appaloosa. Big
gray horse from your pasture."

He had seen the tracks but he did not believe it.
He had not seen them clearly enough, or so he told
himself, and that big gray was not really his . . . It belonged to Bess, and had rarely been ridden by anyone
else.

What Big Injun was thinking, he knew not. To
many Indians the white man's way was incomprehen-
sible, anyway, and this might be just one thing more.
Actually, Big Injun troubled himself very little with
the concerns of the white man. The old ways were
gone, and he had adjusted himself as well as might be.
His own lands, or those of his people, lay far away to
the east. And they had been driven from them by other
Indians before ever the white man came. Soon his
people had learned where the power lay, and he had
in his own way accommodated himself to the future.

He was asked to sit in the jail from time to time, to
track . . . which he loved doing . . . and he ate well,

slept in a comfortable bed, and led a life of relaxed comfort. And if this was so, it was because of Borden Chantry, who had first made a place for Big Injun on his ranch. Then, when the freeze-up killed his stock, Chantry had brought Big Injun along when he came to town.

His horse . . . the big gray. Borden Chantry stared out the window at nothing.

The gray had been in the pasture. And of course, a number of people might have roped the horse, but not many could ride it. The gray loved Bess, but was notoriously edgy with anyone else, and would pitch violently if straddled by anyone she did not know.

This was a fact known to just about everyone in town. And it was highly unlikely such a person would attempt to ride a horse of such temperament when riding on a killing mission.

Big Injun rarely volunteered anything. He did so now. "Man ride him," he said.

Chantry turned his head and looked at the Indian. "A *man?*"

"Big man . . . heavy."

Big Injun would know that from the tracks, and a good tracker could judge very well when a horse carried a heavy man.

"As big as me?"

"Maybe bigger."

Borden Chantry got slowly to his feet. He took out his six-shooter and spun the cylinder. Then he dropped it in its holster, and he did not put the thong back in place.

He went out into the street and stood there for a long time. Then he walked across to Reardon's saloon, and after a bit, down to Henry's, then to the Mexican café. Only then did he return to the Bon-Ton.

"When I was gone yesterday," he suggested, "was anybody around asking for me?"

"No . . ." Ed shook his head. "Dot worked part of the day, but things was quiet. Prissy was in, but you were out of town and Lang didn't come around . . . Nobody asked for you, Marshal."

"Thanks." He sat down at the table near the window

and thought about Hyatt Johnson, then about George
Blazer. He was still thinking about each person, checking what he knew against time and place, when Ed
called out.

"Marshal? I forgot. Blossom Galey was in. She asked
for you. Wanted to know where you were, when you'd
be back."

Blossom Galey . . . She had been born in this town,
and had lived most of her life on the ranch. Hyatt
Johnson traveled a good bit, but . . . .

"Marshal? Look yonder!"

A man had walked his horse up to the hitching rail
and swung down. He was lean and tall, carried himself
very straight, and he had a dark, handsome face under
his black, flat-brimmed hat. He wore a jacket of buckskin, but it was a short, Spanish-style jacket. He also
wore a pistol.

Borden Chantry said, "Ed? Ask that man to come in
and have a cup of coffee with me?"

Ed went to the door and spoke. The man looked
around, nodded, then tied his horse. It was a buckskin,
and a fine animal. Kim Baca had better not see that
one, he told himself. He might even forget his resolution
about not stealing from a Sackett.

The man stepped in, paused, then walked over.
"Marshal? I am Tyrel Sackett."

"Sit down. I am afraid I have some bad news for
you."

Then, quietly, Chantry told him what he had learned.
Of Joe Sackett's arrival in town, his visit to Mary Ann
Haley, to the bank, his stop at the hotel, and his return
to Haley's. And also of the brief fight with Kerns and
Hurley, so far as he knew of it.

"Then the man who killed my brother is still loose?"

"He is . . . but not for long."

"You know who he is?"

"I do."

"Then why isn't he in jail?"

"You can help me, Sackett. I need to know a few
things from you that might help. I haven't made any
arrest because I have had to work this out carefully.
Your brother's murder was only one of several."

"You are sure it was murder?"

"There's no doubt. And the man who did it is in town now . . . or was a short time ago.

"Sackett, you come from Mora. You've lived there awhile?"

"I have."

"Do you know of any man wanted for murder or some other serious crime from your area?"

"Not right now. There've been some shootings, but most of them came out of land grant fights, or just simple arguments over cattle or cards."

"About seven years ago . . . maybe eight. You were marshal there yourself for awhile, I think."

Sackett stared out the window, then shook his head. "Nothing my family was involved in, nothing I can recall."

"Know a cowhand named Pin Dover?"

"Sure. He worked for me. He was a good hand."

"Did anything happen while he was in the country? Any unsolved murder, robbery, anything of the sort?"

"No . . . no, I can't think of anything. Of course, there was the Mason case, but that came to nothing."

"Tell me about it."

"There was a girl in Las Vegas . . . I've forgotten her name . . . very attractive, though. Her father ran several thousand head of cattle over there. And on the stage from St. Louis, she became acquainted with a man named Ford Mason. He was a good-looking man, carried himself well, and represented himself as a former officer in the cavalry, now a businessman.

"He had a way with horses, seemed to be able to handle the worst of them. And he did some trading around the country while he and this girl became better and better acquainted.

"There was a stage robbery about that time, and it carried a shipment of money from the bank, some of which had been paid into the bank by the girl's father. Shortly after, Ford Mason bought a drink for the father . . . his name was Cunningham, I recall . . . and Cunningham recognized the gold eagle that paid for the drinks as one he had deposited in the bank.

"He knew the coin because of two small notches cut

into it just below the date. Of course, he said nothing, but it started him thinking, and he wrote to a friend of his in the War Department.

"No officer named Ford Mason was known, but the description answered that of a deserter who had since been involved in a bank robbery with Langdon Moore, a man named Wells, and a Charley Adams.

"Cunningham faced Mason with the facts, and there was a shooting. Cunningham was severely wounded and his daughter shot through the arm . . . I am sure that was accidental. In any event, Ford Mason skipped the country, and Miss Cunningham talked her father into dropping the charges."

Borden Chantry listened without comment. The story was not an unfamiliar one. In the west, the man who sat beside you on a stage or in a restaurant might be a prince or a thief, and nobody was inclined to ask questions. Each man was accepted as he represented himself unless he showed himself to be otherwise.

"Are you staying in town, Sackett?"

"You say my brother was buried? Is there a marker on the grave?"

"Not yet," Chantry shifted uncomfortably. "You see, when we buried him we didn't know who he was. We'd have marked the grave, though."

"Thank you." Sackett got to his feet. "I shall handle that myself. Having been an officer, I understand your problems, but if there is anything we can do, please let us know."

He paused. "You understand, Marshal, we want the killer brought to justice. In fact, we insist upon it. If it turns out that you cannot find him, we would have to take steps.

"I'm not shipping cattle this year, so I've a few months to spare, and when my time runs out, there are always Bob, Tell and Orrin.

"Then I've some kinfolk here and there about the country, and they have a little time they can spare now and again. It might take a year, even two or three. But we'd sort of stay with it, Marshal. If it took five years or even ten . . . Or twenty, we'd still be sort of meanderin' around, lookin' into things."

"Bye an' bye one of us would come up with him, somewhere, sometime."

"You want to move the body?"

"My brother's? No. My ol' pappy used to say, 'Let the chips lay where they fall,' and we reckon that's the way to do it. There've been a sight of Sacketts buried across the country, an' most of them are buried where they fell. So we'll leave Joe right there where you put him, only we'll leave a marker on the grave so's someday folks will know where he staked his last claim."

Tyrel Sackett walked out the door and Borden Chantry sat alone, the cold coffee in his cup forgotten.

Now he knew, and now he had it to do. And he did not relish the job.

He went around the corner and on to his own home and opened the gate. For a moment he stood there, looking at the small white house. Only a rented house, but it had been their home. And Tom would remember this when even the ranch was forgotten—and the cave Tom had discovered by the spring.

He went inside and went to the wall and took down his spare gun and checked it. Then he thrust it behind his belt. Bess stared at him, her eyes wide and frightened. "Is there trouble, Borden?"

"I am hoping there won't be. I shall be making an arrest now."

"Be careful, Borden."

"That I'll be, but he's a foolish man. He's killed six men to cover up a crime for which no one wanted him. And I do not doubt he'll be foolish still."

"Borden? Who is it?"

He lifted a hand. "Wait, Bess. I do not want to say the name until I must. Have a warm supper for me, Bess, I'll be wanting it."

He walked outside and closed the gate carefully behind him. And then he walked, in long strides, toward the street.

Chapter XIX

A half hour earlier, Kim Baca had got up from his chair and put down the magazine he had been reading. He saw a shadow near the door, and when he stepped into the doorway he found a gun in his belly.

He knew the man by sight, but had never known his name. But there was no question about the gun. It was a Colt .44, a weapon with considerable authority.

He backed into the office. "What's the idea?"

"Get back into that cell," the man said quietly, "and you'll live to hear the story. One yip out of you, and you won't."

"Ought to be a good story, but I got an idea who'll write the end to it."

"Just get back into the cell. Besides, if you yelled, the first man through that door would be Chantry and he would be dead before you could tell him why."

He closed and locked the cell, then stepped over to Boone Silva's cell and opened it. "Your clothes are in the outer office, in the closet. Your gun is there, too, but in case you might prefer it, I brought you this."

It was a heavy express shotgun, double-barreled. It would be loaded with heavy slugs.

Then the man put a small sack of gold pieces on the desk. "There's three hundred. Here's an order on our friend for the rest. Now go do the job you were hired for."

Boone Silva looked at the money, then at the man who was paying him. "When?" he asked.

"Now . . . this minute. He'll be coming here, and I want him dead, *dead* . . . Do you hear?"

"I hear." Silva looked at the money again. Somehow it did not seem very much for a man's life. Yet Chantry had arrested him, and paraded him through the street in his underwear. And for that there had to be a killing or he'd have to find a far country, far from here, far from everywhere that he knew. For such a story has wings.

"All right," he said, but the man was gone.

Boone Silva dressed quickly, surely. He belted on his gun, spun the cylinder. He glanced at the shotgun, and hesitated.

"Silva," Baca said, "open this cell, will you?"

"Go to hell," Silva replied conversationally.

"You're a fool if you go against him. There isn't a man living who can get lead into him without taking just as much. That's a tough man, Silva, a very tough man, and he won't hesitate. He's doing what's right, and he knows it."

"I'll kill him, then I'll ride."

"How far? A mile? Ten miles? A hundred miles? Do you know who rode into town today? Tyrel Sackett. *Tyrel,* did you get that? He took Cruz, he took Tom Sunday, he's taken the best of them. Boone, if you get that marshal, Tye Sackett waits on the other side of him. And if you should get Tye, there's Tell.

"Take my advice, Silva, grab yourself a horse and ride. He won't stop you. He's got other things on his mind, and he never wanted you, anyway.

"Ride! Ride, Silva, while there's time."

"I took his money."

"To hell with the money! He'll be dead within the week."

Boone Silva turned toward the cell, shocked. "What do you think I am, a *thief?* When you take a man's money, you do the work he paid you for!"

He looked again at the shotgun. His every instinct told him to take it, but his pride rebelled. No man alive could draw as fast or shoot as straight as he, and he was not about to back down to any country marshal, nor did he need any margin. He would meet him on his own ground, on his own terms.

There was also a measure of wisdom eating into his zone of madness . . . To shoot a man in a gun battle with pistols was one thing, but a shotgun looked like murder—and could mean hanging!

He stepped out into the street.

A few steps away, a team of mustangs stood at the

hitch rail, heads hanging, drowsing in the sunlight. Further along, at Time Reardon's Corral and at Henry's, several saddle horses stood, awaiting their masters' pleasure.

Lucy Marie was standing in front of a store window, looking at something.

One by one, his eyes picked out the doorways, studying each in turn . . . No sign of Borden Chantry.

From talk around the jail, he gathered that Chantry favored the Bon-Ton, which was just beyond the post office. He scanned the street again, disappointed that there was no sign of Borden Chantry.

As he started to walk, he drew abreast of the post office and saw the postmistress staring at him, her mouth open with surprise.

Grimly, he told himself that a lot of people were going to be surprised, especially that town clown, that small-town marshal, that—

"Looking for me, Boone?"

He had stepped past the post office corner and was opposite the gap that separated it from the Bon-Ton. A right-handed man can fire easier to the left than to the right, and Boone Silva knew it. But Chantry was on his right, and he swung his right foot back to bring him face to face with Chantry. His right foot came down and he fired.

The quick turn, Chantry's coolness, and some sneaking inner doubt of his own wisdom conspired to make him miss. The shot went high, grazing the lobe of the marshal's ear. The marshal was looking right at him, both eyes open. Then his gun stabbed flame, and Boone Silva caught one where it mattered.

It was a little low, but the blow of the bullet strike was enough to make him stagger. Staggering, Silva missed his second shot. He never got a third one.

Suddenly he was on his knees. He had no idea how he got there. Angrily he started to get up, but there was something wrong with his legs. He couldn't draw either one from beneath him.

He tried again, but somehow his legs had gone nerveless. And then he was lying with his face in the dust. He tried to push himself up.

He looked, and Borden Chantry was standing there, gun in hand, just looking at him, and waiting.

Waiting for what?

His eyes misted over and he swore at himself. What was going wrong with his eyes? At a time like this? He made it to his knees. Then after an effort, he got one leg underneath him.

"You should have stayed where I left you, Boone," Chantry said.

There were others standing around now. Boone Silva could hear the shuffle of their feet, the rustle of their clothing, the creaking of the boardwalk.

"It didn't have to be this way," Chantry continued. "I put you away for safekeeping."

"I'd taken his money." Boone was anxious for Chantry to understand. After all, Chantry had played fair with him. "I had it to do. You understand that, don't you?"

"Of course."

Boone Silva raised his hand to fire . . . and there was no gun there.

He stared at it, puzzled. Then he looked at the ground. And it lay there in the dust by a bit of bunch-grass. He reached out for it and his face hit the dust again. Something welled up in his throat and he coughed . . . blood. It was blood . . . his blood.

He was dying.

No!

He thought he screamed the word, but the sound was only inside. With one great spasmodic contraction of muscles, he lunged to his feet.

He! Boone Silva! To die? *No!* He lunged forward and then he fell, and that time he lay still.

Across the street at the Corral, somebody started playing the piano to get the crowd back inside. The last sound that came to his ears was that piano, playing a tin-pan, jangling accompaniment to his dying.

Borden Chantry thumbed a cartridge into the chamber from which he'd ejected the empty. Then he holstered his gun.

Big Injun was there.

"Take care of him, will you? And when you've taken

him away, bring my horse and ask Bess to pack some grub. I'll be gone for awhile."

He went back to the jail then, and let Kim Baca out of his cell.

"He wouldn't listen, Chantry. I tried to tell him. He said he had it to do. Can you understand that?"

"I can, and so can you. Every man has his own sense of what is honorable, Kim. That was his."

"It was the other one let him out. I wasn't expecting anything like that, Marshal. I never had a chance."

"You're just lucky he didn't want to alarm the town, or he would have killed you. I'm going up to the house, but it won't matter much, because he'll be gone."

"You think he's running?"

"He was running when he came here, Kim, and he will always be running. He killed six men because he thought somebody was hunting him, and nobody was. Once you get the law on your trail, there's just no place to rest."

Blossom Galey was standing in front of the Bon-Ton. She looked empty and old.

"Has he gone, Bord?"

"I think so, Blossom. You were too good a woman for him, anyway."

"Maybe . . . maybe. But I need a man, Bord, I want to be a woman again. George knew, and he tried to warn me. He was riding to tell me again when he got killed. I know that, and I guess I always knew. But he was a smooth-talking man, and he said the words I wanted to hear. It wasn't him. It wasn't Lang Adams, it was those damn stupid words! I'm a lonely woman, Bord, an' I'm not a kid any more. And I don't like riding range and laying out work for the hands.

"I'd like to have a kid of my own, and I'd like to get up at ten o'clock and read a newspaper or sew. But I helped run the ranch for Pa, and then I ran a bigger ranch for my first husband, an'—"

"Take a walk over and see Bess. She'll be alone, too, for a few days now. You go see her. I'll just go off up to Lang's and see if he's around."

"He's gone. I knew he was a light man, I knew it all the while. There was no weight to him, Bord. Not like Pa, or you, or old George Riggin. He was an easy-talking man, an' he was damn good-lookin', but there was no bottom to him, no stamina. I knew it all the time. My common sense kept tellin' me the truth and my heart kept listening to the words. Bord, I—"

"Go along to Bess now, Blossom. She's been wanting to see you."

- "All right, Bord. All right." She turned away, then stopped. "You be careful now, d'you hear? He's a damn fine shot with any kind of a weapon. That ol' fifty-two was Pa's. I never thought of it until yesterday, an' when I went to look in the attic, it was gone. But he's got him a Winchester now, Bord, an' more'n two hundred rounds for it. You be careful."

Borden Chantry walked up the outside stair of the apartment above the store. He knew Lang Adams wouldn't be there, but he had to look.

It was a neat enough room, but too much flim-flammery to suit Chantry. On the table there was a note.

Dear Bord:
   Don't come after me. I am leaving the country and you will see me no more, so let it lay. I was the best pete-man in the country until I thought I'd marry rich and settle down, and it got me nothing but trouble. I am going back east now and take up where I left off. You stay off my trail. I never wanted to kill you, I never did. You were the closest thing to a friend I ever had.

                              Lang

And signed below it, still lower on the page, *Ford Mason*.

"But you killed six men, murdered them. Six good men, who had lives of their own to live. You took those lives away, Lang, and left them with nothing. And Billy McCoy without a dad. Old Helen Riggin to live out her days alone. And Pin Dover's woman, wherever she is."

He spoke aloud, to an empty room, and then he turned and pulled the door quietly shut behind him and went down the steps.

Blazer came to the foot of the steps. "If it's Lang, Bord, I saw him leave town. He rode out east."

"Thanks, George." Chantry eased his gun on his hip. "You know, George, Lang should have stayed back east where he came from. He lived out west eight or nine years and never learned a damn thing."

"Maybe," Blazer said, "but you be careful. He won half the turkey shoots in the county with that rifle of his, and there's a lot of open country between here and Carson."

"He hasn't gone to Carson," Chantry said patiently. "He's gone west. Right now he's headed for Denver or Leadville, and maybe later to San Francisco."

The Appaloosa was saddled, the saddlebags and canteen were full. Borden Chantry walked into the office and stuffed a handful of cartridges into his pocket. The loops in his belt were already full.

"Marshal?" Kim Baca got up quickly. "How's about me ridin' along? I'm good on the trail, like you know, and—"

"You stay here, Kim. Keep an eye on things. Anything you don't know about, ask Big Injun. He knows more about the job than I do."

He took a spare badge from the desk drawer. "Wear this until I get back. Anything needs doing, you do it."

Kim Baca flushed. "Now, see here, Marshal! I—"

"Do what you're told, Baca. I'll be back."

He stepped into the saddle and walked the Appaloosa over to his own house. Bess came out, Tom and Billy with her.

"Boys, you take care of Ma, d' you hear?"

"Sure, but can't we—"

"Borden? Do you have to go?"

"I do."

"Then come back. I'll keep Blossom here with me. We'll be company for each other."

He kissed her lightly, and turned the Appaloosa into the trail.

Lang had some good traits, but basically, he was a thief. Now what would a thief be likely to do when he figured he was leaving the country for good? Even if he had some money?

He'd try to steal some more, some he happened to know was where it was.

Borden Chantry hoped he would be wrong. And he hoped he would not pick up the trail where he thought it would be. But he was not wrong, and the trail was there.

Chapter XX

The sky above was red and the sand below was pink, and Borden Chantry rode a trail between—a trail where a man could die.

The leather of his saddle was like the leather of his cheek. And he sang the song of Brennan as he rode, of *Brennan on the Moor,* the Irish highwayman who rode a robber's trail in a land quite far from his

He wasted no time in scouting. He looked not once toward the east, for Lang had known how to find Boone Silva. And such a man would ride westward to escape, westward to the broken country of the Cimarron, to the Mesa de Maya, Sierra Grande and the place called Robbers' Roost, or even to the town of Madison where the outlaws came to carouse and drink.

It was a wild and lonely land cut deep by canyons, ribbed with red rock walls and dotted with crumbling mesas, black-topped with lava from fires burned long ago. Among the red walls and the crumbling lava blocks were the greens of piñon, pine and juniper, and here and there, if a man but knew, there was water enough and plenty.

He rode the blue roan Appaloosa with a splash of dotted white across the hips, a horse that loved a trail through wild country and kept its ears pricked for the crossing of each ridge, the turning of the bend.

The cicadas sang in the brush, and the air was hot and still. And high above the land, a buzzard swung in lazy circles down the evening sky, secure in the knowledge that where men will ride, men will die, and content to await their dying. From all earthly troubles the buzzard was aloof, untouched by wrangle and debate, the song of bullet or the whine of arrow, the pounding hoofs, the sudden fall, the choking thirst or the flaming heat. He had only to bend a dark wing where the sky hung its clouds against the sun, and to await the inevitable end.

Borden Chantry was riding in his own country, in wild country. He liked the movement of his horse, the feel of it between his knees, he liked the trickle of sweat down his cheek. He liked squinting against the sun, the creak of saddle leather and at night the wolf howl against the moon.

He held to low ground and took his time. The Appaloosa was a good trail horse, blending well with the terrain and with a liking for rough country and hard work.

The trails he rode were the trails left by buffalo, used occasionally by wild mustangs. He made no attempt to find and follow the trail left by Lang Adams, for the trails of men in a western land are apt to be channeled by their needs. Water, food, and companionship of their kind—these are the things that make trails converge.

Lang Adams was not a western man, but he had been a hunted man. And a hunted man is like a hunted wolf or any other animal, and he would be wary. Not only would he be wary, but he would be ready and waiting to kill. And Lang Adams had wasted no lead on the men he had killed. His work had been done with neatness and precision—and with utter ruthlessness. So far as Borden Chantry knew, Lang Adams had never missed a shot.

Somewhere up ahead, somewhere not very far off, Lang would be waiting. He might hope that Boone Silva had done his work, but he might lay other, similar plans. Just as Chantry knew something about the manner of man Lang was, Lang knew as much or more about him. Lang had reason for concealing himself from others, Chantry was a frank and open man.

He veered suddenly to the south, crossing the bed of Carrizo Creek and following it back toward the east for a half mile before emerging among some rocks and low brush. He scanned the country, then rode on and fell into an old Indian trail, well-worn but long unused. He cut to right and left but found no tracks.

The Old Santa Fe Trail lay off to the south, a day or two days' ride ... He did not know how far, only that it lay there. Long abandoned now, it was only a maze of ruts cut deep into the earth. Six thousand wagons and sixty thousand mules had used that trail annually, and enough men to people a good-sized town had traveled over it every year. He had always told himself he would someday ride south and see it, but he never had. There had always been work to do.

Several times he cut to right and left to check for tracks, but found none. He seemed to be riding alone in a lonely land. When he found the stone house, he was surprised.

It was empty, long abandoned. He tried the windlass in the well and brought up some water. After he had pulled several buckets, he let his horse drink, then pulled another and drank himself.

He lifted the latch and opened the door. Pack-rats had been there, but they had abandoned it, too. He took the dried wood from their nest and built a fire in the chimney, made coffee and fried some bacon. He ate part of the lunch Bess had put up for him and then he moved outside and bedded down under the stars.

By daybreak he had been two hours in the saddle. He was deep in the winding canyons of the Mesa de Maya, and by mid-afternoon he was watering his horse in the Cimarron near the western end of Black Mesa.

He had crossed the river and was coming out of the water on the far side when he saw the track.

He recognized it at once. Lang Adams' big black. The tracks were no more than an hour old.

Chantry turned abruptly, and at a canter rode his horse east a short distance, hit an old trail going up an intermittent stream and followed it into the broken country beyond. He watched for sign, saw none, and guessed that Lang had gone up the Cimarron, a safe guide toward the west.

Robbers' Roost lay east, but Madison was west, and a more likely spot for Lang, anyway. Borden Chantry had no intention of riding into Robbers' Roost. He was after but one outlaw, and had no intentions of trying to shoot his way through the bunch that hung out at Coe's place.

He kept to the canyons and mesas, saw no tracks, and came within sight of the Cimarron only occasionally. By nightfall his best guess put him twenty-five to thirty miles east of Madison.

Choosing a place on the lee side of a leaning juniper, he put together a quick fire of dry sticks. There was little smoke—that little dissipated by passing through the foliage of the juniper. He ate another of the sandwiches Bess had made, then packed his gear and rode on for more than a mile before he found what he wanted. Staking the Appaloosa on some grass, he moved up to a ledge slightly above the horse, and went to sleep.

He wanted, if possible, to make his arrest without shooting. He had no desire to kill any man, let alone one who had but recently been a friend.

How he was to bring this about, he had no idea.

It was sundown on the following day when he rode into Madison from the south. He had cut away from the Cimarron and reached the trail somewhat north of the towering peak known as Sierra Grande.

There were but half a dozen buildings scattered along the street, and several houses and cabins clustered or scattered where convenience had chosen the spot. There were three corrals within sight; none of them held a black horse. There was what appeared to be a stable, and a dozen horses were tied at the hitching rail in front of what appeared to be a saloon.

The sun was down but there was still a red glow on the crest of Emery Peak, named for Madison Emery— for whom the town was also named.

Without a doubt, some of the horses belonged to outlaws from the Roost, and he would find no friends among them. Nor anywhere in town unless it was Devoy, whom he had heard was a good man. Yet he had no desire to put any of them in a position of helping the law. His was the job to do, and he was asking no help.

A lot of men had died, and Lang had attempted to kill him.

He dismounted and stood for a moment in the darkness beside his horse, considering his next step. He had no desire to be shot down as he entered the saloon. Yet he was tired, hungry, and irritable because of it.

He stood for a moment, and was just about to step up on the walk when a man came out of the saloon, walked to the edge of the porch and stretched. Then he saw Borden Chantry, a dark figure looming in the gray light near his horse. The man's arms came down slowly.

"You don't have to get edgy," Chantry commented, "I'm not hunting you."

"That's a comfort." The man's voice was amused. "I just had me one drink too many and my shooting might not be so good."

"Where can a man put up his horse and get some grub?"

"You can get the grub inside. The horse you'll have to take yonder to the stable, unless you want to chance the town corral. I might add that the town corral is the first place a man runs to when he needs a horse bad . . . And mostly they aren't choosy about whose horse they take."

Chantry chuckled. "I set store by mine," he said. "He's carried me a far piece."

"Put him in the stable. Cost you fifty cents and worth it. Nobody touches them horses, as riders hereabouts know their welcome would run out mighty fast."

He seemed to be trying to see Chantry in the dark. "Do I know you?" he asked suddenly.

"Doubt it. I've heard of this place, but was never here before."

"That's the way it is with most of us. This place is off-course for the law, so we set about and cut a few whing-dings or whatever you call it.

"Good booze," he added, "if you're a drinker. I'm not, but a man was buying and I had a couple. Isn't often you find a live one around here."

"Big handsome man? Just rode in?"

"Seems about right. Talks mighty easy, and carries a rifle as well as a six-gun. Makes me think he might be expectin' trouble. Are you it?"

"Might be, although I'm hoping there won't be any." Chantry paused a moment. "Knowing you're feelin' queasy, I hate to tell you this, but I'm the law."

"You come to the wrong place, Law. Was I you I'd put old Ap there between my knees and show some dust."

"You know, that's right good advice. I just wish I could take it. One thing you might spread around, though. And that is that I'm not looking for anybody else, or noticing anybody but one man.

"It's not just a matter of law. This gent shot at me here and there. Makes me nervous, a feller shooting at me like that—especially from cover. Figured the only way I could get over that nervousness was to sort of round him up and put him away somewheres.

"I might add that that man I'm huntin' killed a Sackett, and ol' Tyrel, he's back over in my town right now waitin' to see if I bring him back. If I don't, he and some of his kinfolk might ride right down here and see if this place will burn—and how many of you boys will fight to keep it from burning."

"We ain't likely to scare very easy, Mister Chantry. None of us boys are. However, none of us are feelin' warlike here at the moment. Also, Logan Sackett was in camp awhile back, and somehow or other I do believe folks like to leave him alone. He struck me as a a man with a rough edge on him.

"Who'd you say you wanted? Was he ridin' a black horse? Big man?"

"Sounds like him. I knew him as Lang Adams, but that wasn't really his name. Back east . . . he's an eastern thief, anyway, not western . . . back east, some knew him as Ford Mason."

"Well, now. I'm agin that. We've enough broke outlaws out here now without havin' that eastern labor come in to take the bread an' butter right out of our mouths.

"Yes, that man is in there right now. Not in the saloon rightly, but in a room at the back of the bar, eatin' by hisself. He sets facin' the door with a rifle on the table and a six-shooter in his holster."

"Fine." Chantry paused just a moment. "Friend, I'm going to put my horse in the stable. You go in there and order me some supper and when it's ready, you have it taken right back to that room and put it on the table in front of him. You needn't tell him who's going to eat with him, but I'll be right in."

When he had put his horse in a stall with enough hay to keep him busy, Borden Chantry took the thong off his six-shooter and kept his Winchester in his left hand.

When he pushed open the saloon door and stepped in, all eyes turned toward him. A man in a white apron was just coming from behind the bar with a slab of meat, some beans and bread on a plate. He started toward the opened door of the back room and walked in, putting the plate on the table.

"What the hell?" It was Lang's voice and he was angry. "Damn it, I said I wanted to be alone! Now you get that damn—"

Borden stepped into the door. "Now, that's unkind, Lang," he said quietly. "You never acted that way before."

"You, is it? Damn you, Bord, I told you not to follow me!"

"Lang, it's my job. It's what those people pay me for. I never figured to be very good at it, but you know how it is . . . It's a living."

Coolly, he pulled back a chair and sat down, laying his rifle across one knee, his left hand on the action.

"You travel fast, Lang. Never figured I'd have to come so far. I kind of expected you to wait for me."

Lang stared at him, angry, yet alert for any chance. "We've been friends, Bord. No reason why we have to have trouble just because the folks back in that town got all worked up. If you had just let that body be buried the way you found it, none of this would have happened. I told you that you were taking this job too seriously."

"It's a fault . . . People pay me for a job, I have to do it. Boone Silva felt the same way."

"Boone? What happened to Boone?"

"You wasted your money, Lang. He just wasn't the man for the job."

"I was told he was the fastest—"

"That's what he thought, Lang. But fast is relative, you know. Maybe he was a right fast man where he came from, but this here's a big country."

Borden Chantry picked up his cup with his right hand. "I've got to take you back for trial, Lang. Of course, you're a good talker and, too, if you get a good lawyer you might get off."

Lang stared at him. "Bord, sometimes I don't know whether you're a very smart man or a damn fool."

"More than likely I'm the fool. I just sort of make out around, Lang. But you see, I need this job. My folks would go hungry without it, and now I've got Billy to feed, too . . . It takes money, Lang."

Lang's tongue touched his lips. His right hand was on the very edge of the table. "How about money, Bord? I'm not holding much, but I could stake you. And when the store is sold, there'll be some coming from that . . . Nobody needs to know you ever found me."

"Lang, if I took money from you I'd be a worse man than Boone Silva. In his own way, you know, he was an honest man, and he tried to do what you paid him for."

"What happened?"

Borden gestured casually. "Like I said, fast is relative. He led with a six and I played an ace. It was a showdown and he just didn't have any more cards."

Lang's tongue touched the lips. His eyes were very bright, and there was almost a taunt on his lips and he leaned forward just a little.

"What was it, Lang? How'd it happen with Sackett?"

Lang shrugged. "I managed to be in the kitchen when the coffee was poured. I slipped him a mickey.

Then when he left, I followed him. Lucy Marie tried to get him to come back and sleep there, and she worried me there for a bit. But he wanted to go on to the hotel.

"By the time he got back of the Corral, he was ready to fall, and I was coming up behind him. Just then, some drunken miner in front of the Mex café started to fire off his pistol, so I shot Sackett.

"I picked him up and took his buckskin coat which he'd been carrying over his arm, and took him into the old Simmons barn. I'd just finished swapping shirts with him when he started to come out of it and I had to shoot him again. Then I got his coat on, and put on his shirt . . . it was too small for me, though . . . and went on home."

"Why did you do it?"

"Why? Are you crazy? He was hunting me. He was hunting me for that shooting down below when I killed old Cunningham."

For once Borden Chantry was pleased with what he had to do. "No, Lang," he said quietly, "Sackett wasn't looking for you. Nobody was. Cunningham did not die, and his daughter talked him out of preferring charges.

"Lang, you were the damn fool. You killed all those people for nothing. You were running scared and nobody was chasing you."

"You're a liar!"

"No, Lang. I am not a liar. That is the way it was. George Riggin figured it out, and he was going to tell Blossom to stay away from you. Then you killed him.

"You made every mistake in the book. When you cut that brand away, I knew it had to mean something. But what you didn't guess was that people in a western town notice brands. I just had to keep prying until I found someone who had seen that one."

Both of Lang's hands were above the table edge, and he was smiling—that brilliant, boyish, friendly smile that people liked so well, and that he knew they liked.

"Well, Bord, I guess this is good-bye, isn't it? I'm sorry you had the long ride for nothing."

His left hand dropped suddenly, grabbing Borden Chantry's right wrist while his own right hand went for his gun.

Borden did not struggle. He looked right into Lang's eyes until the gun muzzle was coming over the edge of the table, and then he shot him.

The Winchester muzzle was within inches of Lang's belly when the shot squeezed off, and instantly Chantry lunged to his feet, shoving the table hard against Lang Adams. And as the bigger man fell back, Borden Chantry worked the lever on his Winchester and stood looking down at Lang.

With a casual boot, he kicked the gun from Lang's hand.

Several men came into the door, watching. Lang stared up at him. "Damn you, Bord! You were always a damn fool! You were never smart! You could have . . . Why, I'd have given you five hundred dollars just to ride home! You damn fool, you—!"

His hand went to his belt. "Look, damn you, I've got—"

Borden Chantry felt only pity then. "Lang . . . you've got nothing. Nothing at all. Not even time."

There was a moment then, when he seemed to know. "Bord!" he begged. "Please, I—"

Borden Chantry stepped back and looked at the men in the doorway. "I am sorry, gentlemen. As I said, it was a personal matter."

Over the back of Lang's chair had been hanging a pair of saddlebags. Chantry picked them up. On the bag was burned with a branding-iron ED G—Ed Galey.

Lang's last theft . . . the little money he knew Blossom kept in the house.

In the saddlebag was the small leather sack with several gold pieces. Sackett's gold.

"There's money on him," Chantry said. "Quite a lot, I think. Take it, bury him decent, and split it among you."

"What name shall we use?" It was the stocky outlaw he had talked to out front.

"Ford Mason . . . Lang Adams . . . Whatever you

will. Names meant nothing to him when he was alive, and they mean nothing to him now."

He was five miles up the trail toward home when he realized that he was broke, his horse was tired, and he hadn't even eaten.

ABOUT THE AUTHOR

LOUIS L'AMOUR, born Louis Dearborn L'Amour, is of French-Irish descent. Although Mr. L'Amour claims his writing began as a "spur-of-the-moment thing," prompted by friends who relished his verbal tales of the West, he comes by his talent honestly. A frontiersman by heritage (his grandfather was scalped by the Sioux), and a universal man by experience, Louis L'Amour lives the life of his fictional heroes. Since leaving his native Jamestown, North Dakota, at the age of fifteen, he's been a longshoreman, lumberjack, elephant handler, hay shocker, flume builder, fruit picker, and an officer on tank destroyers during World War II. And he's written four hundred short stories and over fifty books (including a volume of poetry).

Mr. L'Amour has lectured widely, traveled the West thoroughly, studied archaeology, compiled biographies of over one thousand Western gunfighters, and read prodigiously (his library holds more than two thousand volumes). And he's watched thirty-one of his westerns as movies. He's circled the world on a freighter, mined in the West, sailed a dhow on the Red Sea, been shipwrecked in the West Indies, stranded in the Mojave Desert. He's won fifty-one of fifty-nine fights as a professional boxer and pinch-hit for Dorothy Kilgallen when she was on vacation from her column. Since 1816, thirty-three members of his family have been writers. And, he says, "I could sit in the middle of Sunset Boulevard and write with my typewriter on my knees; temperamental I am not."

Mr. L'Amour is re-creating an 1865 Western town, christened Shalako, where the borders of Utah, Arizona, New Mexico, and Colorado meet. Historically authentic from whistle to well, it will be a live, operating town, as well as a movie location and tourist attraction.

Mr. L'Amour now lives in Los Angeles with his wife Kathy, who helps with the enormous amount of research he does for his books. Soon, Mr. L'Amour hopes, the children (Beau and Angelique) will be helping too.

BANTAM'S #1
ALL-TIME BESTSELLING AUTHOR
AMERICA'S FAVORITE WESTERN WRITER

☐	13561	THE STRONG SHALL LIVE	$1.95
☐	12354	BENDIGO SHAFTER	$2.25
☐	13881	THE KEY-LOCK MAN	$1.95
☐	13719	RADIGAN	$1.95
☐	13609	WAR PARTY	$1.95
☐	13882	KIOWA TRAIL	$1.95
☐	13683	THE BURNING HILLS	$1.95
☐	12064	SHALAKO	$1.75
☐	13680	KILRONE	$1.95
☐	13794	THE RIDER OF LOST CREEK	$1.95
☐	13798	CALLAGHEN	$1.95
☐	14114	THE QUICK AND THE DEAD	$1.95
☐	14219	OVER ON THE DRY SIDE	$1.95
☐	13722	DOWN THE LONG HILLS	$1.95
☐	14316	WESTWARD THE TIDE	$1.95
☐	12043	KID RODELO	$1.75
☐	14104	BROKEN GUN	$1.95
☐	13898	WHERE THE LONG GRASS BLOWS	$1.95
☐	12519	HOW THE WEST WAS WON	$1.75

Buy them at your local bookstore or use this handy coupon for ordering: